"Yo, Tameka!"

Tameka looked up. Lacey was smirking at her. Then a splash of cold water hit Tameka right between the eyes. For a split second Tameka was angry, but then she realized the water felt incredibly refreshing.

"Thank you! Now take that!" Tameka yelled as she tossed the contents of her cup toward Lacey.

Lacey ducked—and the water hit Sheila and Geena instead.

"You missed me! You missed me!" Lacey sang out.

Sheila was holding a small bottle of carbonated water, which she shook up and aimed at Tameka. The water went everywhere.

All this happened in a few seconds—about the amount of time it took Mrs. Essex to back out of the way.

Mr. Thomas wasn't as fast. He got splattered when Rory shook up *her* water and aimed it at Kyoto.

"That's enough!" Mr. Thomas hollered.

Tameka began sneaking up on Lacey from behind.

"Tameka! Ann! Thomas!" Mr. Thomas bellowed. "I said, *that's enough!"*

Lottery Blues

by

Emily Costello

A SKYLARK BOOK

NEW YORK · TORONTO · LONDON · SYDNEY · AUCKLAND

For Laura Blake Peterson,
an important member of my team

RL 5, 008–012

LOTTERY BLUES

A Bantam Skylark Book / November 1998

Skylark Books is a registered trademark of Bantam Books, a division of Bantam Doubleday Dell Publishing Group, Inc. Registered in U.S. Patent and Trademark Office and elsewhere.

ISBN 0-553-48648-9

Published simultaneously in the United States and Canada.

Bantam Books are published by Bantam Books, a division of Bantam Doubleday Dell Publishing Group, Inc. Its trademark, consisting of the words "Bantam Books" and the portrayal of a rooster, is Registered in U.S. Patent and Trademark Office and in other countries. Marca Registrada. Bantam Books, 1540 Broadway, New York, New York 10036.

PRINTED IN THE UNITED STATES OF AMERICA

OPM   0   9   8   7   6   5   4   3   2   1

chapter 1

TAMEKA THOMAS TRAPPED THE SOCCER ball with her thigh. She waited for it to hit the ground and stopped it with the bottom of her left cleat. Using her right foot, she scooped the ball toward Tess Adams.

Tess jumped backward, getting her foot up high and kicking the ball in midair. Her aim was perfect. The ball zoomed straight toward Yasmine Madrigal's head.

Yasmine watched the ball approaching, her face set in a grimace. At the last second she stepped forward and whacked it with her forehead.

"Ow," Yasmine moaned.

Tameka caught the ball. "Did that hurt?"

1

Yasmine made a face, rubbing her forehead. "Yeah." Then she smiled. "But not *too* much. Let me try that again."

"No, it's my turn," Tess said. "Meeki, toss me the ball."

Tameka threw the ball. But her aim was way off. "Sorry," she said. "I wasn't paying attention."

Tess ran after the ball, catching it just before it disappeared into the jungly underbrush in the woods behind her house. "You'd better start concentrating. I'll be mad if you space out during an important play."

Tameka shrugged. "You may not care," she said. "We could end up on different teams this season. If we do, you'll be praying I snooze through every game."

That Friday evening—only two days away—the American Youth Soccer Organization in Tameka's town was holding its annual lottery. All the coaches would meet to pick their teams for the next two seasons—the entire school year.

Tameka loved her old team, the Stars, and she didn't want to lose it.

Tess kicked the ball to Yasmine, who half-heartedly passed it back. "I can't believe the coaches are going to break up the Stars."

The ball came to Tameka, and she kicked it to Tess. "I wish we could *do* something to keep the team together."

"Like what?" Tess asked.

"You could talk to your dad," Yasmine told Tameka.

Tameka's dad was the Stars' assistant coach. He tended to stay in the background, letting the girls' head coach, Marina Santana, make most of the decisions for the team. Still, Tameka was sure Marina respected his opinion.

"I'll talk to him," Tameka promised. "And I think we should get the team together on lottery night. That way nobody will have to wait for the news alone. Can you come over Friday?"

"Sure," Yasmine replied.

"Sounds fun," Tess said.

"Great!" Tameka tapped the soccer ball to stop it, and passed it back to Yasmine.

"Do you guys want to go back-to-school shopping tomorrow?" Tess asked. "It will get our minds off the lottery. And besides, we've got less than a week of summer vacation left."

"Count me in," Yasmine said. "All my clothes look *so* sixth grade."

"I guess I'll go too." Tameka shrugged.

Tess made a face. "Are you sure? Maybe you'd prefer to walk over burning coals. Or get your braids caught in a fan."

Tameka sighed. "Sorry. I just wish this summer would last another eighteen years." She usually liked school. But this year would be different. For the first time since second grade, Tameka was going to be in a different class than Tess.

Tess was entering the Gifted and Talented class—a special program for the school's Great Brains. Tameka was worried Tess would find her new classmates more interesting than her old ungifted and untalented friends. Plus the whole situation was a big blow to Tameka's ego. If the school separated out all the gifted and talented kids, who was left? *The stupid and inept,* Tameka thought. *In other words, me.*

★

"I love back-to-school shopping," Nicole Philips-Smith told Geena Di Gregorio. She held a lime-green sweater up to her chest and made a supermodel pout. "What do you think?"

"That sweater is great," Geena replied. "And I don't blame you for liking back-to-school shopping. Unlike *some* people, you don't have to wear a uniform to school every day."

Nicole gave Geena a sympathetic smile. Geena went to Catholic school, and her uniform *was* ugly.

"Maybe you can buy some new *after*-school clothes. I'm sure I'm going to be invited to loads of parties this year. You can come along."

"Whoa! Am I hearing things, or did you just nominate yourself Most Popular Girl in the Seventh Grade?"

"I can't help it," Nicole said. "This school year is going to be great for me. I'm going to be the student council president, the most important seventh-grader at Country Day."

"I'm honored to know you, Your Highness. Just don't forget who helped you get elected."

"Thank you, Geena," Nicole said piously.

Geena *had* been a big help during the election, Nicole thought as she headed toward the register with the sweater. Nicole's archenemy,

Sheila McGarth, had come *this* close to winning. But then Geena and Nicole had found a videotape showing Sheila viciously kicking one of the Stars during a game. As soon as the kids at school saw it, Sheila's chances in the election were history.

Result: Nicole was elected. Now she looking forward to the best school year ever. Nothing could ruin it.

★

"Hello?"

"Rose, hey. It's Tameka."

"Hi, Tameka. What's up?"

"I'm having a party for the Stars tomorrow night. We're going to wait for the results of the AYSO lottery together. You have to come."

"Are you sure? I mean, I'm not playing this year."

Tameka blinked in surprise. Between camp and vacations, she'd only seen Rose a couple of times over the summer. Rose hadn't told her she was quitting soccer!

"Why not?" Tameka hated the idea of Rose dropping off the team. The Stars wouldn't be the same without her freckle-covered face—and her habit of ducking whenever the ball got too close.

"Well, you remember that I play the violin, right?" Rose sounded excited.

"Yeah."

"I got invited to join the Beachside Youth Orchestra! It's a big honor. We get to travel all over the state to perform."

"What does that have to do with soccer? You can do both."

"Actually, I can't. Orchestra rehearsals are on Saturday afternoon. I'd miss all the games."

"Did you tell the orchestra people you have a conflict? Maybe you can get the rehearsal time moved."

"They wouldn't change the time just for me. Two hundred kids play in this orchestra."

Tameka's mind raced. Somehow she had to convince Rose to stay on the Stars. Maybe if Rose spent time with her old teammates, she'd remember how much fun the team was and realize she couldn't quit.

"Come to the party anyway," Tameka begged.

"Okay," Rose said. "Seeing everyone would be fun."

"Great," Tameka said. She could tell Rose was already having second thoughts about giving up soccer.

★

The next afternoon Tameka was jogging with her father at Lake Shore Park, a narrow strip of grass and sand that ran along Lake Michigan.

Tameka glanced at her dad. The skin on his face was shiny with sweat, and his T-shirt had a damp V in front. He was making a lot of noise breathing, gulping air in through his mouth and pushing it out of his nose.

"Want to slow down?" Tameka asked.

Mr. Thomas shook his head. He never spoke much while he jogged. Probably because he didn't have any air to spare.

Tameka and her dad had been jogging together every evening for almost a month. Mr. Thomas said he wanted to actually work out with the Stars that fall, so Tameka had offered to help him get in shape. She was proud of the progress he'd made. On their first night out, he'd quit after five minutes. Now he could run three miles without stopping.

"Dad, the lottery is tomorrow," Tameka said.

Mr. Thomas grunted.

"Please try to keep the Stars together. I mean, I know Marina will be choosing the players. But I'm sure she'll be interested in your opinion. And we all really want to be together again this season."

Mr. Thomas nodded without speaking. His eyes were fixed on a park bench that was coming up on the right. It marked the end of their run, and it was only about fifty yards away. Tameka put on a burst of speed, finishing at a sprint. Then she jogged in place and waited for her dad to trot up.

The moment Mr. Thomas drew even with the bench, he stopped dead. He put his hands on his knees, huffing for breath. Then he reached for the bottle of water that was attached to his belt and emptied it over his head.

"Good job!" Tameka told him. "But don't stop now. Your muscles will knot up. Keep walking. Come on."

Mr. Thomas reluctantly started to move. He wiped his forehead on his sleeve.

"So, Dad, about the Stars . . ."

"I'll try to keep you and your friends together." Mr. Thomas spoke slowly as he fought to catch his breath. "But the team is going to change . . . at least a little. That's why we have the lottery. To

9

make sure you have the opportunity . . . to play with lots of different kids."

Tameka sighed. Her father saw the lottery as a way for her to make new friends. She saw it as a way of losing *old* ones. Tameka liked all her teammates. She hated the idea of losing any of them. Especially Tess.

chapter 2

"THIS IS SO WEIRD," TESS WHISPERED to Tameka at her lottery party on Friday night. "Everyone looks different."

Tameka let her gaze wander over the girls gathered in her living room. The Stars were standing in groups of two or three, talking and eating pepperoni pizza.

"Yaz looks the same," Tameka said, referring to Yasmine Madrigal. "Same black ponytail—"

"She doesn't count," Tess interrupted. "We've seen her practically every day over the summer. But I haven't seen some of the Stars for months. Did you check out Rose? She got her braces off!"

"I know. She looks so pretty."

"How about Nicole?"

"Total sun goddess." Nicole had clearly spent the entire summer outdoors, probably on her father's sailboat. Her blond hair was bleached almost white, and her skin was tanned the color of honey.

"Geena's cast is gone," Tess said.

"Amber's hair is longer."

"Jordan got some cool glasses."

"And look at Lacey and Fiona, over by the sodas."

Lacey Essex had grown at least two inches in the past few months. She was now a head taller than Fiona. And Fiona . . . well, she wasn't taller or fatter or thinner or curvier, but Tameka still thought she looked older.

Geena came up to Tameka. "Thanks for the party."

"No prob," Tameka said. "Anything for the Stars."

"I hope they don't split us up," Geena said.

"I was just thinking the same thing," Tameka said.

"Me too," Tess added. "Hey—I know! Maybe

we should channel all our positive energy." She put down her drink and motioned for everyone to form a circle. "Join hands!" she ordered.

"What's going on?" Lacey asked.

"The lottery—*that's* what's going on!" Tess said dramatically. She grabbed Tameka's and Yasmine's hands. "At this very moment the coaches are deciding our fate," she said in a hushed voice. "So I want everyone to close their eyes and think positive thoughts. Imagine the Stars together again."

Tameka closed her eyes. *Please let us stay together,* she wished.

An hour passed. The girls finished the pizza. Tameka popped in a video and they lounged around—half watching, half talking. Then Tameka heard the sound she'd been waiting for: her dad's car turning into the driveway.

"Meeki, your dad is home!" Tess said.

Tameka's heart seemed to stop and then start beating at twice the usual speed. Everyone grew quiet—tense, waiting. Tameka switched off the TV as her father came through the door. *This is it,* she thought. *We're about to find out if the Stars get to stick together.*

"Daddy?" Tameka said fearfully. "How did it go?"

"Great!"

Tameka felt every muscle in her body relax. She glanced at Tess. "Great" had to mean the Stars were still a team!

"Yeah, I think we have a terrific lineup," Mr. Thomas said enthusiastically. "Oh, and you'll all be happy to know that we get to keep our name. After a *very* long debate, we decided to let the team names stay with the coaching staff. At first—"

"So we're still together?" Nicole interrupted.

Mr. Thomas turned to Nicole. "Not *all* of you. Rich Slater—remember him from last season?"

"Of course!" Tess said impatiently. "He coaches the Galaxy."

"Right." Mr. Thomas crossed to the table and picked up a glass. He didn't seem to realize a roomful of people was hanging on his every word.

"Apparently Rich's team was weak in the midfield last season," Mr. Thomas said with his back to the room. "So he snapped up Jordan and Amber."

Amber slumped on the couch and dropped her head into her hands.

Jordan's face fell. Tears welled up in her eyes and began rolling down her cheeks. Tameka felt numb as she hurried over to give Jordan a hug. *What's so great about this?* she wondered. *The Stars won't be the Stars without Amber and Jordan.*

Mr. Thomas poured himself a soda. Since his back was turned, he didn't realize the effect his words were having. "One of you guys is going to be a Satellite. Um . . . Sarah."

"No fair!" Sarah wailed. "I'm the *only* one? I'm going to be totally alone?"

Mr. Thomas turned around, looking astonished. "There's no need to get so upset. I'm sure you'll know lots of the girls on the Satellites from last season. And some of them must go to school with you."

"Daddy!" Tameka was embarrassed by how insensitive her father was being. Didn't he know how awful it was to be separated from your friends?

Grown-ups were always changing kids' classes,

changing their teams. "Make new friends," they said. Tameka didn't understand what was wrong with *old* friends. How would the grown-ups like it if kids forced them to quit their jobs so that they could meet new people?

By now the entire team had huddled around Sarah, Jordan, and Amber.

"I—I guess this must be hard on you girls." Mr. Thomas seemed to be choosing his words carefully. "But let me just say one thing. I truly believe the lottery is one of the things that makes AYSO so special. You guys know that playing against a team that's much better than yours—or much worse—is no fun. The lottery balances the teams out. And that makes every game exciting to play. Nothing could be more important."

Tameka knew her dad was right. Balanced teams were important. And she felt lucky to still be on a team with Tess and Yaz. But the Stars *were* losing four players. And right now all Tameka could think about was how much she'd miss them.

★

"I feel so sorry for you," Nicole told Jordan.

Jordan had stopped crying. But she was still sniffling, and her face looked blotchy. She forced a smile. "I'm just glad *you* didn't end up on the Galaxy. I mean, it would have been great to have you on my team, but . . . well, you know what I mean."

"Yeah." Nicole's biggest enemy in the world played for the Galaxy—Sheila McGarth, the girl who'd run against her in the student council election.

Geena was standing behind Nicole. "Maybe you won't have Sheila to worry about," she told Jordan. "She might not even be on the Galaxy anymore."

"In my dreams," Jordan said.

Geena's comment made Nicole think of something important. The Stars were losing Jordan, Amber, Rose, and Sarah. That meant they were also *gaining* four new players.

"I wonder who the new Stars are," Nicole said. "Maybe we know them."

"Let's find out," Geena said.

Geena and Nicole jumped up and headed over to where Mr. Thomas was talking to Tameka and Sarah.

"Excuse me," Nicole said politely. "Do you have a list of the new team members?"

"Sure." Mr. Thomas pulled a list out of his

pocket and handed it to Nicole. Tameka, Tess, Lacey, Fiona, and Yasmine gathered around.

"Did we get anybody decent?" Tess asked.

"Tess!" Tameka gave her a dirty look.

"Sor-ree!"

"Um . . ." Nicole scanned the handwritten names, looking for ones she didn't know. "Here's one, Kyoto Fun-a-ki," she read carefully. "Do any of you guys know her?"

The others shook their heads.

"I think she just moved to Beachside," Mr. Thomas put in. "We got a note from her coach in California."

"Who else?" Tess asked eagerly.

"Yardley Gallagher," Nicole read.

"I know her." Lacey spoke up. "She was in my kindergarten class."

"What's she like?" Fiona asked.

Lacey shrugged. "Last time I saw her, she liked finger painting and jungle gyms."

"With any luck, she's matured," Tess said. "Who else?"

Nicole looked down at the list. The next few names were familiar old Stars. But what she saw written near the bottom made her gasp. "You guys are not going to believe this!"

"What?" Tameka asked.

Nicole swallowed hard. What she had just read was almost too horrible to say out loud. "Sheila McGarth is a Star. And so is her best friend, Rory Carver."

GO TO SLEEP, TAMEKA ORDERED HERSELF the night before the first day of school. She started counting backward from 100, and got all the way to zero without feeling the least bit sleepy.

She sighed, rolled over, and stared at her clock. The numbers glowed in the dark: 12:33.

I have to get up in six hours, she thought. *I'm going to be dead tired tomorrow. I'm going to fall asleep during attendance and make my teacher hate me forever.*

A car came down the street, and Tameka stared at the shadows moving across her ceiling. Starting tomorrow morning she wouldn't be able to pretend things at school hadn't changed. Tomorrow

Tess would disappear into the Gifted and Talented class—and a whole new world. Stupid and inept Tameka and Yasmine would be left behind to start a new grade without her.

And then, after school, the Stars would have a preseason meeting. But it wouldn't be the old Stars—where Tameka had felt comfortable and important. It would be the *changed* Stars. Maybe the new Stars wouldn't like Tameka. Or maybe they'd all play much better than she did, and laugh every time she got the ball.

Tameka had been happy with school and soccer the way they were. *Why can't things stay the same?* she wondered. *Why can't I go back to when I thought Tess would be my best friend forever?* She made a promise to herself. A promise to hold on to Tess and all her old friends as long as possible. She wouldn't let things change without a fight.

"You're late," Tess greeted Tameka the following morning.

"I know. I overslept."

Tess was standing on her front porch, wearing new jeans and a T-shirt she'd bought back-to-school shopping. She was holding a tidy brown-bag lunch and a new notebook. She jogged down her steps and joined Tameka on the sidewalk. They started toward the Madrigals'.

"Are you excited about the first day of school?" Tess asked.

"Oh yeah. Yippee. Can't wait."

Tess gave Tameka a shove. "Well, *I'm* scared to death. What if Hollinsworth finds out I'm an idiot?" Mr. Hollinsworth taught the Gifted and Talented class.

"Fat chance," Tameka said. But she felt better knowing that Tess was nervous too. Her own stomach was twisted in an anxious knot.

When they got to the Madrigals', Tameka ran up the steps and banged on the door.

Yasmine appeared almost immediately. "How does my hair look?" she demanded.

Tameka shrugged. "Curly."

"I know that! I just spent an hour with my mother's curling iron. But does it look curly good or curly bad?"

"Yaz, cut it out!" Tess said. "You sound like Lacey."

"I just want to make a good first impression on my new classmates."

Tameka smiled to herself. Yasmine sounded almost as nervous as she felt. She was glad Yasmine was going to be in her class. At least *both* her best friends weren't gifted and talented.

The girls joked around the rest of the way to school. But when they reached the school yard, Tess grew somber. "I'm not sure when my class has lunch," she said. "But if I don't see you then, wait for me on the steps so we can walk home together."

"Sure thing," Yasmine said.

Tameka felt like hugging Tess and telling her everything was going to be all right. But that was silly. Tess was ten times braver than she was.

"See you." Tess gave them a little wave, took a deep breath, and marched off in the direction of Mr. Hollinsworth's class.

Yasmine grabbed Tameka's arm. "Come on. I want to get seats together."

Tameka and Yasmine scurried down the noisy, crowded hallway to their class. They found two seats in the middle of the room. The classroom clock above the blackboard clicked to 8:15. As if on cue, a woman walked into the room.

"Hello, class!" she said. "My name is Mrs. Keene."

She went to the blackboard and wrote her name in big block letters. Mrs. Keene had pale skin and shiny brown hair pulled into a neat bun. She wore a skirt, stockings, and a white blouse.

"Let's see who's here today," she said brightly. She opened a book and started to take attendance.

After reading a few names, Mrs. Keene frowned at her roll book. "Kyoto Funaki," she pronounced carefully. "Did I say that correctly?"

"Sure," came a voice from near the back.

Yasmine and Tameka traded looks. Kyoto Funaki? That was one of the names from their team list! While Mrs. Keene continued to take attendance, Tameka turned around so that she could see Kyoto. Yasmine looked too.

Kyoto was a tiny black-haired girl wearing a hand-painted T-shirt, black leggings, and dangling earrings. She had her legs crossed on her chair and was doodling with a green pen.

"She looks cool," Yasmine whispered.

Kyoto seemed to realize someone was staring at her. She glanced up and smiled.

Tameka quickly turned back toward the front of the room.

"She seems nice," Yasmine whispered. "Maybe we should ask her to eat lunch with us."

"No!"

Yasmine glanced at Mrs. Keene. She was writing the class schedule on the board and didn't seem to mind that they were whispering. "What's wrong with you?"

"Nothing." Tameka scrunched down in her seat. "I just don't want to be friends with the new Stars."

"Whatever," Yasmine said.

Tameka could tell Yasmine thought she was being silly. Maybe she was. But she couldn't help feeling as if the new Stars were somehow responsible for breaking up the old team she loved.

★

"Hey, Nicole!"

"Hey."

"Hi, Nicki!"

"Hi."

"Nicole, I love your backpack."

"Thanks."

This is great, Nicole thought as she moved down the hallway at Country Day Academy. Practically everyone she passed said hello to her—

and why not? She was now president of the student council. In other words, hot stuff.

She glanced at the big hall clock. There were still two minutes before the start of homeroom—enough time to slip into the bathroom and check her hair and lip gloss. *The most powerful girl in school should look perfect,* Nicole thought.

Nicole pushed through the swinging door and headed straight for the sinks. But she stopped dead when she saw the two girls who were standing in front of the mirrors: Sheila and Rory.

The previous school year, the sight of Sheila had made Nicole jittery. But Sheila didn't scare her anymore. In fact, Nicole was glad she'd run into Sheila. She wanted to talk to her about the Stars.

Nicole was still shocked that Sheila and Rory had both ended up on her team. At the lottery party, Mr. Thomas had explained that Sheila and Rory were both strong defensive players—which was just what the Stars needed now that Rose, Amber, Jordan, and Sarah were leaving. Nicole wanted a balanced team. But *not* if it meant playing with Sheila and Rory.

Sheila and Rory spotted Nicole. They exchanged looks in the mirror and slowly turned to face her.

"I heard you guys are supposed to be Stars this season," Nicole said coldly. "I want you to quit."

"Quit soccer?" Sheila shook her glossy black curls. "Not happening."

"Fine." Nicole felt her anger bloom. "Just don't expect to ever touch the ball in a game. The Stars will *never* accept you as a teammate."

"Why not?" Sheila looked defiant. As usual, Rory stayed silent, letting Sheila do the talking.

"Everyone on the team saw the videotape of you kicking Fiona," Nicole said. As if Sheila could forget. That tape had cost her the election.

Sheila shrugged. "So things got a little rough in the middle of a game. Big deal. There's nothing wrong with playing aggressively."

Nicole rolled her eyes. "That wasn't aggressive. It was mean. And how about the way you broke Geena's arm? Do you really think the Stars will like you after that?"

Sheila turned around to face the mirror. She fluffed up her bangs. "I don't see that it's any business of yours. And *I'm* not worried."

"Well, you should be."

Sheila smiled. "By the end of the first game, I'll have more friends on the team than you do. Guaranteed."

Nicole laughed. "Want to bet?"

"Definitely," Sheila said, sticking out her hand.

Nicole reached out to shake, but snatched her hand back at the last moment. "Wait . . . what are we betting, exactly?"

"That in two weeks, your friends will like me better than you."

"And how do you plan to prove *that*?"

Sheila considered. "Here's how. We'll each have a party on the evening of the Stars' first game. Whoever has more Stars at her party wins."

"What if my parents won't let me have a party that night?" Nicole asked.

Sheila gave a lazy shrug. "Then you lose."

Nicole bit her lip. She had a hundred other questions about how the bet would work. But she knew asking would make her sound weak and worried.

"What does the winner get?" Rory asked.

Sheila slowly ran her eyes over Nicole's new green sweater, an amused smile playing around her lips. "The loser has to wear any outfit the winner chooses, all day at school and to soccer practice."

"I don't know." Nicole could just imagine what Sheila would make her wear if she lost.

Sheila shrugged that infuriating shrug. "Really? I thought I was letting you off easy. I mean, if you're willing to be seen in *that*"—she nodded toward Nicole's new sweater—"then you must not be too particular about how you look."

Rory chuckled softly.

Nicole drew herself up as tall as she could. Why should she worry about this bet? She couldn't possibly lose. The Stars wouldn't even *consider* going to Sheila's party.

She held out her hand. "Fine."

This time Sheila hesitated. "One more thing. You can't tell any of your little friends on the Stars about this bet. That would give you an unfair advantage. And besides, I don't want the whole team jabbering about it. If the coach finds out, she might shut us down."

Nicole considered. "But Rory knows. And two against one isn't fair."

"Okay, you can tell one friend."

"Fine."

Nicole and Sheila shook.

chapter 4

"HERE SHE COMES," TAMEKA SAID EA-
gerly. She and Yasmine were sitting on the steps
in front of Beachside Middle School, waiting
for Tess just as they'd promised. Tameka almost
expected Tess to come out of the building surrounded by gifted and talented Great Brains. She
was relieved to see that her friend was alone.

Tameka jumped to her feet, then pulled Yasmine up.

"Hi!" Tess called cheerfully.

"Hi. How was Hollinsworth's class?"

"Pretty good." Tess shifted the enormous stack
of books she was carrying. "I'm sorry I missed you

guys at lunch. Hollinsworth had us out in the woods, choosing trees to adopt."

"Why?"

Tess waved away Tameka's question. "Don't ask. The important thing is that I may be able to eat with you tomorrow. So, are you ready to go? I'm starving."

"Ready!" Yasmine skipped backward a few steps, and the girls started off for home.

"Why don't you guys come to my house for a snack?" Tess suggested. "Then we can practice our heading some more."

"The snack sounds good," Yasmine agreed. "But no more heading. I need all my brain cells to deal with seventh-grade math."

"Tell me about it!" Tess exclaimed. "Pre-algebra is so weird. What's up with all those X's and Y's?"

"Prealgebra?" Tameka repeated. "What's that? Our textbook is called advanced math."

"Oh." Tess looked embarrassed, and she fell silent.

Tameka suddenly realized why. Hollinsworth's students were taking a different kind of math—

something the teachers figured she was too stupid to understand.

That is so unfair, Tameka thought. *Math is one of my best subjects.* She even explained things to Tess once in a while.

"Guess what?" Tess asked abruptly. "One of the new Stars is in my class."

"Ours too!" Yasmine exclaimed. "Kyoto."

"What's she like?" Tess demanded.

Yasmine shrugged. "I thought she looked cool. But Tameka wouldn't eat lunch with her. So who knows?"

Tess frowned at Tameka for a second but didn't ask any questions. "Well, Yardley Gallagher is in my class. Everyone calls her Yard because she's about three feet taller than a normal kid our age. She's as skinny as a yardstick too!"

"Doesn't sound like she'll be much use on the field," Tameka said.

Tess shrugged. "I don't know about that. I mean, we had lunch together and she told me she's never played before—"

"You hate new players!" Yasmine cut in.

"True," Tess admitted. "But I figured we'd end up with at least one. And if we had to have one,

Yard is probably a pretty lucky draw. I mean, she may be built like a stork, but at least she's smart."

Tameka was a little hurt that Tess had eaten with a new Star. "How smart?" she asked.

"Scary smart." Tess made it sound like a compliment.

Tameka felt as if someone had punched her in the stomach. She could tell that Tess liked Yardley. She'd already made a new friend in Hollinsworth's class.

Yaz and I are toast, Tameka thought.

★

"I've got to throw the coolest party ever," Nicole told Geena that afternoon. "I want people begging me to come."

"What's going to make it cool?" Geena wiggled her toes deeper into the sandbox sand.

Geena's sister Isabella stopped pushing her dump truck through the sand and gave her a puzzled look. "Not cool, Gee. Hot!"

"That's right, Izzie! It *is* hot." Geena turned and smiled wearily at Nicole. "Mom says it hit ninety-two degrees today. My school was an *oven.*"

"We have air-conditioning."

Nicole had taken the bus to Geena's as soon as

school let out that afternoon. She needed to talk to Geena about her party *immediately*.

But she'd found Geena baby-sitting for her two-year-old sister. Isabella needed to be entertained every second. So Geena and Nicole had brought her into the backyard and plopped her in the sandbox. As long as she was happy, they could talk.

Isabella was filling her dump truck with sand and then dumping it. Fill, dump. Fill, dump. She clearly thought this was fun stuff.

Nicole took a sip of her ice water. "Everything about it will be cool. I want the coolest possible food. What do you think? Barbecue? Pizza? A clambake?"

"Grilling is fun."

"Okay, we'll grill. My brother Tyler just got a new stereo. Maybe he'll let me bring it out to the backyard. And we need a theme! Like, um . . . the first women's World Cup! We could decorate with the flags of all the different countries that will be competing."

"That's kind of cool. Fiona's excited about the World Cup."

"Tess would like a soccer theme too. And I'm actually sort of looking forward to this party!"

Isabella looked up. "Party. I come?"

"No, Izzie. This isn't a party for you."

"I no come?" Isabella pouted.

Nicole gave Geena a triumphant smile. "See? It's working already! People are *begging* to come."

Geena smiled back. "Now you just have to work on some people who are out of diapers."

★

"Hey!" Kyoto exclaimed that evening at the Stars' preseason meeting. "I didn't know you guys were on my soccer team! This is so groovy."

Tameka smiled awkwardly at Kyoto, feeling trapped. The Essexes' living room was full of old Stars—and Tameka would have preferred talking to them.

She looked to Yasmine for help.

But Yasmine was beaming Kyoto a friendly smile. "So what do you think of Mrs. Keene?"

"She's sweet," Kyoto said. "Like my grandmother or something." She turned to Tameka. "I love your braids. They totally remind me of Cobi Jones."

"That's why I wear them!" Tameka was flattered—and surprised. The rest of the Stars liked Cobi, but no one was as big a fan as she was.

"You like Cobi?" Kyoto asked.

"Absolutely. He's the coolest! Did you know he used to be on an AYSO team?"

"Of course!" Kyoto exclaimed. "Have you ever seen him play?"

"Only on TV."

"Too bad. My dad and I saw him with the L.A. Galaxy a few times. And once we waited after the game—and I got his autograph!"

"Get out!"

"I swear. Have you seen his show on MTV?"

"One of them," Tameka said.

"I have tapes," Kyoto said. "You should come over sometime and watch them with me."

"Sounds great!" Tameka said. Then she remembered that she'd promised herself she wouldn't make friends with the new Stars.

"So, do you want to come over Saturday?" Kyoto asked.

Tameka shrugged. "Actually, I think I'm busy."

"How about one day after school?" Kyoto said.

"Maybe . . ." Tameka pretended to be uninterested.

"Well, let me know," Kyoto said with an uncertain frown.

Tameka almost felt sorry for Kyoto. But then she reminded herself Kyoto was a *new* Star—an outsider, a party crasher. *Not* a potential new friend.

★

Nicole was standing with Fiona and Geena, but she was having a hard time concentrating on their conversation. Her attention kept drifting to Sheila and Rory, who were sitting on the couch as if they had every right to be there.

A tiny part of Nicole was uneasy about her bet with Sheila. Actually, a pretty big part. In the student council election, Sheila had been ruthless in her attempt to win. Nicole was braced for another nasty fight, and waiting for it to begin was unnerving. She stared down at her cup of ice and decided to get more soda. The meeting was supposed to have started ten minutes earlier, but Marina hadn't arrived yet.

"I'll be back," Nicole told her friends. She wandered into the kitchen and filled her cup. When she got back into the living room, she saw Sheila standing in front of the couch. She was holding up her hands for attention.

Now what? Nicole wondered.

Sheila cleared her throat. "Excuse me, everyone. May I have your attention, please? Just for a moment?"

Geena slid Nicole a what's-she-up-to? look.

Nicole shrugged and took a sip of her soda.

Sheila cleared her throat as the room quieted down. "I . . ." She paused and took a deep breath. "I just want to say I'm sorry for the way I acted last spring."

Nicole narrowed her eyes. Sheila was making a big production of acting nervous. But Nicole wasn't buying it.

"Fiona, Geena"—Sheila made eye contact with each of them—"you must think I'm a monster or something. The way I treated you last season was so immature. But I've really changed over the summer. I've tried to become a nicer person."

Nicole rolled her eyes. Who was Sheila trying to kid?

"Now that we're teammates, I hope we can start over again," Sheila went on. "And to show how thrilled I am to be a Star, I'm holding a party on the day of our first game. I hope you can all be there!"

Nicole's eyes widened in horror. She hadn't even had a chance to ask her parents if she could have a party. Well, there was no time to worry about that now.

"Wait!" Nicole called out. "Um, I'm having a party that night too. A party for the Stars."

Sheila pretended to be crushed by this news. Her mouth turned down at the corners. Her eyes were sad. She looked like a lost puppy. Nicole felt like stomping on her toes. What a fake!

"Couldn't you have your party another night?" Sheila asked.

"Well, no." Nicole tried to look sympathetic. "See, I've, um, already hired a band."

"Oh." Now Sheila looked like a lost puppy with a piece of glass in her paw.

"Maybe *you* could change the night of *your* party," Nicole suggested.

"I can't," Sheila said. "I've already—well, it's supposed to be a secret. But . . . let's just say I've planned something special."

Nicole shrugged and smiled. "Well, I guess everyone will just have to choose."

"I'm sorry I kept you all waiting," Marina said a few minutes later. She was sitting in a big armchair with the Stars grouped around her. Tameka had picked a spot right in front of Marina's chair. Mr. Thomas and Mrs. Essex were listening from the kitchen doorway.

"We didn't mind waiting," Tameka said. Seeing Marina had cheered her up.

"My responsibilities at the university have changed a little this fall," Marina continued. "My work there has been keeping me super busy for the past few days."

Tameka nodded sympathetically. She knew graduate school was hard. Marina had told the team about it during spring season.

"It's great seeing you all . . ." Marina's voice

trailed off. Tameka saw Marina look at Mr. Thomas. He gave her a reassuring nod.

Tameka got an uneasy feeling in her stomach. Something was going on.

"Saying this is tough," Marina continued. "But I'm afraid I can't coach the Stars this season."

CHAPTER 5

"WHY NOT?" TAMEKA DEMANDED. SHE couldn't believe the Stars were going to lose Marina on top of Rose, Amber, Jordan, and Sarah.

"We need you!" Fiona said.

"Please don't quit," Geena put in.

Marina leaned toward the girls, her expression pained. "Making this decision was *so* hard. I really loved being your coach last season. But I simply don't have the time this semester. Listen, I promise to come to your games as often as possible and cheer you on."

Tameka wanted to argue with Marina, to change her mind somehow. But she couldn't think of what to say. She could tell from Marina's sad expression that she hadn't made her decision lightly.

"So who's going to be our coach?" Tess asked.

Marina smiled slightly. "We have that all worked out. Roger is going to move up to head coach." Roger was Tameka's dad. "And Larissa is going to be your new assistant coach."

"Who's Larissa?" Yasmine asked.

"That's me!" Mrs. Essex waved from her spot near the kitchen. She kind of bounced up and down in her sneakers, and Tameka gave her a smile.

Tameka couldn't help liking Mrs. Essex. She was so different from her own mother, who was very elegant, proper, and strict. Mrs. Essex worked as an aerobics instructor, and Tameka had never seen her wear anything but leotards, sweats, and expensive sneakers. Her blond hair was always pulled up into a high ponytail. She didn't really look much older than Marina.

Marina made eye contact with Tameka's dad. "Roger, would you like to take over now?"

"Sure," Mr. Thomas said smoothly. He switched places with Marina and began telling the Stars when and where their practices would be held.

Tameka wasn't paying much attention. She looked around at her teammates. The old Stars all seemed sad, but they were listening intently to what her dad had to say. They seemed to accept him as their new coach.

Tess leaned over toward Tameka. "Why didn't you tell us Marina was quitting?"

"I didn't know."

"Your dad didn't tell you?"

"No way."

Tess shrugged. But Tameka tuned back in to what her dad was saying, or more precisely, the *way* he was saying it. He seemed perfectly comfortable. As if he'd had plenty of time to prepare.

He knew Marina was quitting, Tameka decided. *And he didn't even tell me!* Tameka's sadness gave way to anger. How could her dad have kept something so important from her?

Tameka could hardly wait for the meeting to end. Her dad had some explaining to do!

"Is anyone hungry?" Mrs. Essex asked after the meeting. "I'd be happy to order a couple of pizzas."

Marina laughed and shook her head. "Thanks,

but I have a paper due on Monday, if you can believe it. I've got to hit the library."

Mrs. Essex gave her a hug. "Good luck. And don't worry about the Stars. We'll take care of them."

"I know." Marina picked up her backpack and started saying goodbye to everyone. Tameka gave her a big hug.

Sheila smiled sweetly at Mrs. Essex. "Thanks so much for the invitation. But I can see my mother's car outside. Rory and I had better go."

Great, Nicole thought. *I can stay.*

"What do you say, girls?" Mr. Thomas asked Tameka, Tess, and Yasmine. "If you want to hang out for a while, that's okay with me."

"No thanks," Tameka said immediately.

"Why not?" Yasmine asked.

"I want to go home," Tameka insisted.

Tess shrugged. "Well, okay. I guess we'll see you guys at the first practice. Bye, Yard."

"Bye!"

"I want to sit in front," Tameka announced as she walked toward the car with Tess, Yasmine, and her dad.

"Fine with me," Yasmine said.

Tameka waited until everyone got into the car and buckled up. Then she asked her dad, "How long have you known that Marina was quitting?"

Mr. Thomas shrugged as he fitted the key into the ignition. "She told me on the day of the lottery."

"Then why didn't you tell me?" Tameka demanded.

"Please don't use that tone of voice."

Tameka took a deep breath, trying to calm down. She didn't get angry very often, and she didn't like it much. It made her feel strangely out of control.

"If you had told me, I could have stopped her," she said.

"I don't think that's very realistic," Mr. Thomas calmly replied. "And besides, it wasn't my news to tell. It was Marina's. Understand?"

Tameka just shrugged. The only thing she understood was that her dad had kept a really big secret from her.

★

As soon as the pizza had been ordered, Lacey led Nicole, Fiona, Geena, Kyoto, and Yardley into the den. "That was a wild team meeting!" she said.

"Did you know your mom was going to be assistant coach?" Fiona asked.

"Nope!"

"Well, I think it's totally cool," Kyoto said. "Lacey, your mom seems *so* nice."

"Thanks."

Nicole noticed how comfortable Kyoto acted with the group of girls she'd never met before. You could tell how self-confident she was by the clothes she wore too. Kyoto had on a patterned red-and-black shirt with a black fleece vest. Her bun was held in place by a comb with a red dragonfly on it. Nobody at Country Day dressed like that, but Nicole had to admit that Kyoto looked fantastic.

"I can't believe Marina is leaving," Geena said. "I'm going to miss her so much."

"Was she a good coach?" Yardley asked.

"The best," Fiona said.

Yardley had stuck around with a bunch of strangers too. Nicole gave her credit for that, but she didn't think Yardley had as much style as Kyoto. Yardley looked somehow out of proportion, Nicole thought. Like a newborn puppy. Her feet were too big, and she always seemed to be tripping over them. Plus none of her clothes fit her properly.

"What was that chick Sheila talking about?" Kyoto asked. "Why was she so, like, 'I'm sorry' and 'I hope we can work together'?"

Nicole leaned forward, eager to tell the story. "Last year, Sheila was on this team called the Galaxy. She was always cheating, and we actually got a tape of her kicking Fiona."

"Really?" Kyoto stared at Fiona, who nodded.

"Yes, and that's not all," Nicole rushed on. "Sheila also broke Geena's arm!"

Now Kyoto's dark eyes were really wide. "On purpose?"

"Yes," Nicole said.

"No," Geena said at almost the same time.

Nicole snapped her attention to Geena. "What do you mean, no?"

Geena squirmed in her chair. "Well, we were playing two-on-two out in the park," she said, addressing Kyoto. "Sheila was playing rough—"

"Too rough," Nicole put in.

"Too rough," Geena said. "But I don't think she actually meant to hurt me."

"Are you mad at her?" Kyoto asked. "I

48

mean . . . she really hurt you, even if it was an accident."

Geena shrugged. "I was for a while. But now I sort of feel like . . . accidents happen."

"Besides," Fiona added, "she said she was sorry."

"Pizza's here!" Lacey's little sister, Cherie, bounced into the room. "Pizza! Pizza! Pizza!"

Lacey immediately stood up. "Great. I'm starving. Come on, I'll get some plates."

Nicole stayed in her seat as the other girls followed Lacey into the kitchen. She was too amazed to move. Fiona was actually ready to accept Sheila's phony apology! And Geena . . . how could she believe that her broken arm was an accident?

When Nicole had made her bet with Sheila, she'd assumed her teammates knew Sheila was a liar. She'd assumed they disliked her as much as she did.

Big miscalculation.

Maybe winning this bet wasn't going to be as easy as she'd imagined.

★

"So who's playing at your party?" A few minutes later, Lacey sat down next to Nicole and put her pizza plate on her knees. Fiona sat on the floor near them.

"Playing?"

Geena nudged Nicole. "You said you were having a band at your party."

"Oh . . . right." Nicole had only said that because it seemed like a good reason why she couldn't change the date. Of course she hadn't *really* hired a band. She hadn't had time. She'd only made her bet with Sheila that morning!

Kyoto and Yardley came out of the kitchen and joined the group.

Lacey gave Nicole a put-out look. "Well, I wish you'd asked me first. You could have had Cole's band, Haz Mat."

"Cole?"

"Lacey's boyfriend," Fiona explained.

"He's not exactly my boyfriend," Lacey said. "We just like hanging out together. And anyway, Fiona's boyfriend is in the band too."

"Josh is not my boyfriend!" Fiona yelled.

Lacey giggled. "Whatever."

Nicole had seen Cole and Josh a few times last season when they'd come to watch the Stars play. They looked nice enough. And besides, if she invited their band to play at her party, Lacey and Fiona would definitely come. *But how can I get*

Cole's band without admitting that I lied during the meeting? Nicole wondered.

"Maybe your boyfriend's band can play at Sheila's party," Kyoto suggested.

Lacey's face brightened. "Cool idea!"

"No it's not!" Nicole said quickly.

"Why not?" Lacey asked. "I thought you already had a band."

"Not exactly." Nicole hesitated, uncertain how to explain this without telling the other girls about her bet with Sheila. "See . . . When Sheila suddenly invited all of you to her party, I had to say something to make *my* party sound cool."

"You lied to us?" Yardley stared at Nicole.

"Sort of." Nicole turned away from Yardley and looked at Lacey. "Will you ask Cole to play for me? I really want him to."

Lacey shrugged. "Sure. Why not?"

Nicole gave Geena a satisfied smile. Suddenly her party was shaping up quite nicely!

★

"This is great," Tameka said on Thursday afternoon. "Just like last year."

She smiled across the table at Tess and Yasmine. That afternoon, Mr. Hollinsworth was allowing his students to eat lunch with the rest of the school. Tameka was glad to see Tess in the middle of the day.

Tess smiled back. Then her gaze shifted to something behind Tameka. "Hey, guys!" Tess called. "Over here."

"Tess!" Tameka protested.

"What?"

But it was too late. Yardley and Kyoto had already seen Tess, and they were coming over to the table. Now Tameka couldn't say she didn't want to eat with them.

Kyoto and Yardley pulled up chairs.

Tameka felt her good mood evaporate.

"You guys shouldn't have taken off so quickly last night," Kyoto said. "We had fun hanging out at Lacey's."

Yard nodded in agreement.

"Nicole told us about Sheila and all the nasty stuff that went down last season," Kyoto said. "It's so weird that you guys are teammates with these chicks who were, like, your mortal enemies last year."

"I think it's more than weird," Tameka said.

"I think it's awful. More proof the lottery is stupid."

"What's the lottery?" Yard asked.

"It's the way AYSO shuffles all the players each fall," Tess explained.

"We have absolutely no control over where we end up," Tameka said. "Sarah, this girl who was on our team last spring, is now on a team where she doesn't know *anybody*."

"The idea is to make sure all the teams are balanced," Kyoto put in.

"It's stupid," Tameka repeated. "It would be much better if teams got to stick together."

"I don't think so," Kyoto said. "I mean, imagine what it would be like if one team was really, really good. Playing against them would be a drag."

"True," Yaz said.

"Have you ever been through a lottery?" Tameka asked Kyoto.

"Nope. I joined AYSO last fall. Then, as soon as school ended in the spring, my dad and I put everything we own into our van and it was good-bye, California!"

"No offense," Tameka said. "But that proves

you have no idea what you're talking about. Trust me, the lottery's dumb."

"But without it, Kyoto and I wouldn't be Stars," Yard pointed out.

"Exactly," Tameka said. "We didn't ask you to barge in."

The other girls grew still.

Kyoto gave Tameka a furious look. "Well, being rude isn't going to change things. You have a new team now. I think you should face facts and get on with your life."

Before Tameka could reply, Kyoto calmly picked up her belongings and moved to another table. Yardley followed. Tess and Yasmine were staring at Tameka as if she had grown another head.

chapter 6

"O'CONNOR RESIDENCE."

"Um, hi. Is Rose there?"

"Just a moment, please."

"Hello?" Rose said a few beats later.

"Hey, it's Tameka."

"Hi! How's it going?"

"Pretty good. Listen, I noticed you didn't come to the team meeting last night. So I thought I'd let you know that the Stars' first practice is this afternoon. If you show up, my dad might find a way to let you play."

Rose was quiet for a long moment. When she did speak, she sounded puzzled. "Tameka, I'm not playing this season. I mean, I'm glad you want me to—but I can't."

"I guess I was hoping you'd change your mind."

Rose laughed. "Well, not yet. But orchestra rehearsals don't start until Saturday. If the conductor is really awful, I might."

Well, Tameka thought. *At least that's something.*

"First practice of the season." Geena took a deep breath and smiled in satisfaction.

Nicole and Geena were standing on one of the Beachside playing fields, waiting for the rest of the team to get there. The sun was beating on Nicole's back, making her feel sticky. She was nervous about practicing with Sheila and Rory. The thought of spending an entire hour with them wasn't exactly thrilling.

"Isn't it great to be back?" Geena asked.

Nicole shifted her weight impatiently. Sometimes she found Geena's endless good mood . . . unrealistic.

"Sure, it's great," Nicole said in an it's-not-great tone. "It's great *if* you don't mind the fact that the two people I hate most in the world are on our team now."

Tess, Tameka, Yasmine, and Mr. Thomas were coming across the field. They looked hot and sweaty.

"Here come some potential party guests," Geena said. "You'd better turn on the charm."

Nicole nodded, feeling a nervous lurch in her stomach. Then she forced herself to smile. "Hey, Yaz!" she called. "You got new cleats."

Yasmine looked down at her feet. "Yeah. Do you like them?"

They were basic black cleats. Nothing special. "They're great!" Nicole said.

Yasmine smiled. "Thanks!"

Nicole's gaze fell on Tess. Could she flatter her in some way? *You're dreaming,* Nicole told herself. She and Tess had never gotten along. Changing that would take more than a few compliments.

Yardley arrived, and Nicole thought she looked uncomfortable and out of place. She was definitely ready to be buttered up. But before Nicole could think of anything nice to say to her, Sheila and Rory came skipping across the field.

"Hey, everyone!" Sheila said brightly. "My mom was worried we'd melt in this heat, so she sent along a bunch of bottles of water. Anybody want one?"

"Me!" Tess said immediately.

"Definitely," Tameka said.

While the rest of the team gathered around Sheila and her mini-cooler, Geena and Nicole exchanged nervous looks. *Cold water on a hot day,* Nicole thought. *The girl is good.*

★

"Okay, girls!" Mrs. Essex called. "Gather around."

Tameka stood between Yasmine and Tess in the circle. She tried not to look at Kyoto, who was directly opposite her. She hadn't spoken to Kyoto since their argument at school that day.

Thinking back on the fight made Tameka mad all over again. How dare Kyoto put down the Stars?

Tameka was in a bad mood anyway. Having practice without Marina, Sarah, Rose, Amber, and Jordan didn't feel right. She wished she could do something to call the whole thing off.

"Here's what we decided," Mrs. Essex was saying. "I'm going to run the warm-ups, since that's something I know a lot about. And since I'm no soccer expert, Roger is going to take care of the rest of the practice."

When did he *become a soccer expert?* Tameka looked at Tess and rolled her eyes. Tess just shrugged.

"Okay, let's start with a hamstring stretch," Mrs. Essex said after the girls had marched in place for several minutes. "Bend at the waist. Keep your back parallel to the ground. Don't lock your knees. Now raise your head."

Tameka raised her head and found herself gazing right into Kyoto's eyes. Meeting Kyoto's gaze made her uncomfortable, so she stood up.

"Is something wrong, Tameka?" Mrs. Essex asked.

"No."

"Then why don't you hold the stretch a little longer?"

Because I don't want to look at Kyoto! Tameka thought. "Because I don't want to," she said out loud.

She felt a tingle in her stomach as she spoke. Tameka was almost always polite to grown-ups, except her parents sometimes. Talking back to Mrs. Essex felt dangerous—and exciting at the same time. Especially since her dad was off setting up cones on the field and couldn't order her to do as she was told.

Now Fiona stood up. "I'm done too," she announced. "That stretch kills the back of my legs."

"That's the idea," Mrs. Essex said mildly.

Fiona shrugged. "Can't we do something else?"

"Well, okay," Mrs. Essex said. "Everyone, why don't you come out of that? Bend at your waist and reach for your toes."

Toe touches sounded good to Tameka. At least during them she wouldn't have to look at Kyoto.

Ten minutes later Mr. Thomas approached the group with a big smile. "Okay, girls, why don't you do a few laps to warm up your muscles? Then we'll do a dribbling drill."

Nicole, Kyoto, Yardley, Geena, Lacey, Sheila, and Rory started to run. The rest of the team hesitated.

"Laps?" Fiona asked in a tone of disbelief.

"Yeah, I figure three or four should be enough to loosen up your muscles."

"But it's so hot," Fiona complained.

"And besides," Tess said, "don't you think we should be doing something that improves our *skills* and not just our *endurance*?"

"Well, I—"

Tameka gave her dad an impatient look. "And

why should we warm up, if we're just going to stand around and wait for our turn to do a drill?"

"I've got the equipment set up, so you won't have to wait," Mr. Thomas said.

"It's still too hot to run laps," Fiona insisted.

Mr. Thomas shrugged. "I'm not going to argue with you. Run the laps if you want. It's up to you."

The girls looked at each other uncertainly.

Tess was the first to decide. She took off for the goal line at a fast pace, obviously trying to catch up with her teammates. Yasmine started after her.

But Fiona flopped down on the ground. Tameka hesitated a second and then sat next to her.

"I miss Marina," Tameka said, loudly enough for her dad to hear. "Unlike *some* people, she always ran a perfect practice."

"We have ten minutes left," Mr. Thomas told the team. "Let's finish up with a scrimmage. I'll play so that we can have even teams. Who would like to volunteer to play goalkeeper?"

"I will," Kyoto said.

Nobody else spoke up.

Geena nudged Nicole with her elbow. "Volunteer!" she whispered.

"Why? I hate playing goalkeeper."

"So does everyone else!"

Oh, right. Nicole suppressed a sigh. Trying to be popular was a drag. "I'll do it," she told Mr. Thomas wearily.

"Great." Mr. Thomas started pulling black pinnies from the equipment bag. He tossed one to Nicole, then continued to hand them out as he assigned positions on the black team. "Geena and Lacey, you guys handle defense. You're going to be our one and only midfielder, Tameka. And Tess and Yardley, try the front line."

Nicole trooped back toward the goal. Once she got there, she turned around and squinted toward the halfway line. Mr. Thomas had a ball tucked under one arm. He was patiently explaining something to Yardley.

I wonder whose party she'll go to, Nicole thought.

Yardley and Tess seemed buddy-buddy. *Yard will probably go wherever Tess goes,* Nicole figured. *And since Tess can't stand me, they'll probably go to Sheila's.*

That gave Sheila two guests. Plus Sheila herself and Rory. That made four.

Who definitely will come to my party? Nicole wondered.

Geena.

Fiona—forgiving Sheila for kicking her was one thing, but going to a party at her house was another.

Add in me, and that gives me three Stars, Nicole thought.

Only three?

Who else? Nicole frantically asked herself.

Tameka, probably. For some reason she'd been snubbing the new Stars. Which was weird because Tameka was usually so friendly. Okay, so that was four. Who was left?

Lacey.

She'll come to my party to see Cole play, Nicole decided.

Kyoto.

Hmmm. That was hard to call. Kyoto was nice to everyone.

Yasmine.

Well, Yaz was good friends with Tess. So maybe she'd want to go to the same party—Sheila's.

On the other hand, Yaz was also friends with

Tameka. *So maybe she'll come to my party with her,* Nicole thought.

Then again, was it realistic to think that Tess and Tameka would split up? They went everywhere together.

Nicole sighed, realizing that it was impossible to guess what all her teammates would do. One thing was certain: She had to be nice to all of them until the night of her party.

chapter 7

TAMEKA SHIFTED HER WEIGHT IMPA-
tiently as her dad told Yardley what attackers were
supposed to do. The lesson had turned into a debate about strategy—which was silly since Yard
couldn't even dribble the ball.

Finally Mr. Thomas called, "Let's get started!"

Yard and Tess lined up on the halfway line.
They were facing Rory and Fiona, who were on
the front line for the other scrimmage team.

Tess passed to Yard.

Yard stood rooted in place, watching the ball
roll toward her. She waited for it to hit her cleats
and then carefully put a foot on it.

Fiona stood a few feet away. For some reason

she didn't steal the ball. *Maybe she feels sorry for Yard,* Tameka thought. *She acting like she's never even watched soccer on TV.*

"What do I do now?" Yard called to Tess.

"If nobody's on you, try to dribble toward our goal!"

Yard pointed to Fiona. "Someone is on me."

"Then pass!" Tess didn't sound so patient anymore.

Yard awkwardly passed the ball in Tess's general direction. But by then Fiona had come out of her daze. She intercepted the slow-moving ball, dribbling it right past Yard.

Watch and learn, Tameka silently told Yard. She ran in front of Fiona, distracting her with some speedy footwork. She drew the ball away from Fiona and dribbled up the right-hand side of the field.

Fiona pounded after her. But Tameka was faster. She dribbled deep into the other team's territory. Then Sheila rushed her from the left. Yaz wasn't far behind.

Tameka spotted an unguarded space on the left side of the field. And Tess was open.

"Coming at you, Adams!" Tameka sent a blistering pass diagonally in front of the goal. Tess put on a burst of speed, catching the ball just in front of the left goalpost. Kyoto hovered a few feet away. With her legs wide and arms outstretched, Kyoto had the left side of the goal well protected.

Tess got her left foot under the ball and booted it just inside the right goalpost.

Kyoto took three long steps. She jumped for the ball. Reaching way above her head, she used her fists to bang it out of the goal. Tameka was stunned to see the ball bouncing back toward her. Kyoto was good!

"Get it, Mr. Thomas!" Sheila yelled. "Kick it out of there!"

Mr. Thomas, who was playing defender, galloped toward the ball.

Tameka got there first. She worked the ball closer to the goal, then hammered it straight in.

Kyoto lunged sideways. She stopped the ball with her belly and held it to her body as she stood up. Another amazing save! Kyoto rolled the ball to Yaz, who dribbled forward a few yards. Yaz passed to Sheila.

Sheila lofted the ball toward the halfway line. Tameka broke into a run.

"That's it for today!" Mr. Thomas called. "I'll see you all back here the same time on Tuesday."

Tameka slowed down.

Tess jogged up to her. The girls headed back toward the sidelines together.

"Can you believe those saves Kyoto made?" Tess asked. "She's fantastic."

"I don't care," Tameka said with an angry shrug of her shoulders. "You were there at lunch. You heard what Kyoto said about the old Stars. After that, I don't see how you could be excited about having her on our team."

"Simple. With Kyoto in the goal, our opponents won't be able to score. And after practicing with her, our shooting skills are going to be awesome!"

"I don't care if she's the next Briana Scurry," Tameka snapped. "I don't like her."

Tess stopped walking and stared at Tameka. "Whoa. Tameka, you like everyone."

"Not Kyoto."

"I'm shocked."

"Well, get ready for another shock. I don't like Yardley either. Why are you being so friendly to her?"

"I—I like her. And she's in my class."

"So?"

"Shhh. Here she comes."

Yardley approached them. "Is there something I could do to improve my skills before the next practice?" she asked. "It seems like I have a lot of catching up to do."

Tameka sighed. That Yardley girl was *such* a Great Brain. She wanted an extra-credit assignment for soccer!

"Sure," Tess said, giving Tameka an uneasy look. "You can practice your ball control. Come on, I'll show you."

Tess and Yardley moved off into the center of the field. Yasmine trailed after them, sipping from a bottle of water. Most of the other girls drifted off toward home.

"Would you mind helping me carry the equipment to the car?" Mr. Thomas called to Tameka.

Yes! Tameka wanted to scream. *I mind! I don't want to pick up balls while Tess plays with her new friend.* But Tameka knew her dad wasn't really *asking.* He was telling.

She was seething as she picked up the net bag

and started toward the parking lot. Having her dad coach the Stars just wasn't working out. Marina had to come back.

★

Marina lived a few miles outside Beachside, near the university. Tameka found her address in the phone book and talked Yasmine into biking out there Saturday morning.

The building turned out to be a big apartment complex that looked a lot like a lakeside motel. Yasmine and Tameka found Marina's apartment and rang her bell.

"Just a sec!" Marina threw open the door and gave them a puzzled smile. "Hi! What are you guys doing here?"

Tameka started to lose her nerve. Seeing Marina at home was weird. She was barefoot, for one thing. And she seemed so much more relaxed than at practices and games.

"It was her idea." Yasmine tilted her head in Tameka's direction. "May I please have a glass of water? It's hot."

"Sure. Come on in."

Tameka followed Yasmine and Marina inside and looked around. The wall-to-wall carpeting was the same blue as the building's exterior walls. A tiny counter connected the kitchen and the living room. It was covered with open textbooks and notebooks.

"Were you studying?" Tameka asked as she perched on the edge of the sofa.

"Yeah. But I don't mind taking a break." Marina dropped some ice into three glasses and filled them with water. She handed one to Yasmine and one to Tameka, keeping the third for herself.

"Thanks." Yasmine took a long drink.

"So . . . how is school going this year?" Marina asked as she sat on one of the stools at the counter.

"Fine," Yasmine said. "But Tameka wants to talk to you about the team."

Marina looked at Tameka and gave her an encouraging smile.

Tameka took a deep breath. "The thing is . . . I really think you should come back."

Marina shook her head. "I'd like to, but I can't. That wouldn't be fair to the team. I'm too busy with school to do a good job coaching."

"But you *have* to," Tameka insisted. "We had our first practice Thursday and it was just *awful*."

"Awful how?" Marina looked sympathetic. And maybe a tiny bit skeptical.

"It was like when you have a sub at school," Tameka said. "Dad and Mrs. Essex don't know what they're doing, and everyone knows it. The first thing Mrs. Essex told us was that she didn't know much about soccer."

"But your dad does."

"Not really! Besides, my dad is totally wishy-washy. When I do something bad at home, my mom punishes me."

Marina didn't look convinced.

Tameka rushed on. "They didn't even make us warm up right. And Fiona is getting away with murder."

Marina swished the water around in her glass, frowning thoughtfully. "I tell you what. I'll stop by your practice on Tuesday."

"To coach?"

"No. But maybe I can give your dad and Mrs. Essex some hints on how to improve practices."

That wasn't exactly what Tameka wanted. But at least it was a start. Maybe once Marina was at the playing fields, Tess or Nicole—or someone—could convince her to stay.

chapter 8

MRS. ESSEX WAS FULL OF PEP AT PRACtice on Tuesday. She seemed unaware that the afternoon was almost unbearably hot and humid.

Tameka was dressed in her lightest clothes, but she still felt sticky. The sky was full of dark, threatening clouds. Tameka prayed they wouldn't let loose until after Marina showed up.

"Let's march in place," Mrs. Essex said brightly. "Get those knees up. Higher! Good. Now plant your feet hips' width apart and get your arms into it. Reach up, up, up, up. Now in front, front, front . . ."

Mr. Thomas was standing next to Tameka, doing the warm-up with the team. Tameka tried not

73

to look at him. She thought he looked silly. His movements were always a beat behind everyone else's. She wished he would give up and stand on the sidelines.

"Now let's turn to the right. Slide your back foot out and try to get your heel on the ground."

"Hey, Marina's here!" Tess called.

Tameka looked up and saw Marina walking toward them from the parking lot. She wasn't wearing her cleats and workout gear the way Tameka had hoped she would. She was walking slowly, as if she felt she didn't belong there.

"Hi, Marina!" Geena called.

Marina waved. "Don't let me interrupt! Just pretend I'm not here."

Mrs. Essex smiled and nodded. "Okay, turn to the front. Your right knee should be bent."

As Tameka stretched, she watched her father straighten up and go to greet Marina. They chatted in low voices, occasionally glancing over at Tameka. Mrs. Essex ignored the interruption, confidently continuing with the warm-up.

"What is Marina doing here?" Tess whispered.

"Checking up on us," Tameka whispered back.

"Why?"

"I asked her to."

"You did?"

"Yeah. I'm trying to get a decent coach for our team."

"Meeki!"

"Okay, now let's stretch out your necks," Mrs. Essex said. "Put your chin to your chest."

Tameka dropped her head and closed her eyes, trying not to think about how shocked Tess looked. She was almost sorry when the stretching ended a few minutes later.

"Okay, Roger!" Mrs. Essex called. "They're all warmed up and ready to go!"

"Coming!" Mr. Thomas said goodbye to Marina and jogged back toward the team. "Okay, girls, we're going to work on your throw-ins. Grab a partner."

Marina motioned for Tameka to join her. Tameka walked over, half expecting Marina to be mad.

"Hi."

"Hi. Why don't you walk me to my car?"

"Okay."

Marina was silent until they got out of earshot

of the rest of the team. "I wanted to tell you I talked to your dad. He and Larissa have things under control. The Stars are going to be just fine."

"I guess."

"Was there some other reason you wanted me to come today?"

Tameka felt so hopeless. Her plan for Marina hadn't worked, and she wasn't sure what to do next. All she knew was that she wanted things to go back to the way they used to be. Back when she thought Tess would be her best friend forever.

"I—I just want the old Stars back," Tameka said. "Everything was so much cooler last season."

Marina gave her a sideways hug. "I know. Change stinks. Especially if you keep thinking about how great things used to be. But maybe something good can come out of it too."

"Like what?"

"I don't know. Maybe Larissa can teach you a fabulous way to stretch your triceps. Or maybe one of your new teammates will become a friend."

Or maybe one of my new teammates will steal my best friend, Tameka thought.

★

Nicole watched as Geena picked up the ball, pulled it back behind her head, then took a step forward and threw. The ball bounced near Geena's feet and rolled back toward her.

"Try again," Nicole called. "You're letting go too late."

Geena frowned with concentration as she picked up the ball. She threw again, making the same mistake she'd made before. The ball landed at almost the identical spot.

"You're still letting go too late," Nicole called.

"Whatever." Geena kicked the ball. "Your turn."

Nicole stopped the ball and picked it up. "Everything is ready for my party. Mom and Dad said it was okay. I ordered the food and drinks. And Lacey promised to call Cole."

"Aren't you going to call him yourself?" Geena squinted. She was facing into the sun.

Nicole tossed the ball from hand to hand. She knew she should call Cole, but she felt funny about it. She didn't have a lot of experience talking to strange boys on the phone.

"I'll call him in a few days," she decided.

★

Tameka watched Marina drive away. Then she reluctantly made her way back to the field. The team had paired off. Mr. Thomas was working with Fiona.

"You're my partner, Tameka!" Lacey called. She had been running the drill with her mom. But now Mrs. Essex tossed the ball to Tameka and headed for the sidelines.

Tameka wasn't usually partners with Lacey. She scanned the field, wondering who Tess was working with. Yaz? No, Yaz was throwing the ball to Kyoto. Tameka spotted Tess near the sidelines. She was carefully showing Yardley how to hold the ball to get the most power behind her throw-in.

Why does Tess have to be partners with her? Tameka wondered. Tess already spent hours with Yardley every day at school. Didn't she ever want to spend time with her old friends?

Part of Tameka realized she was being silly. After all, Tess always helped the worst members on the team. It was just like her to make Yardley her pet project. But still . . .

"What are we supposed to do?" Tameka asked, feeling cranky.

"Get about ten feet away," Lacey said. "We're going to take turns doing throw-ins."

Tameka backed up and tossed the ball to Lacey's feet, being careful to hold the ball in both hands, bring it back behind her head, and keep her feet on the ground. Lacey stopped the ball. She scooped it up and got ready to throw. "What was Marina doing here?"

"Oh, seeing if she could give your mom and my dad some advice."

Lacey threw the ball. "Why?"

"I sort of asked her to." The ball was high and coming fast. Tameka backed up and trapped it with her chest. She let the ball drop and put one foot on top of it.

"You think my mom is a bad coach?" Lacey asked as Tameka picked up the ball.

"I didn't say that!"

"You didn't have to *say* it. I can tell you think it by the way you've been acting."

Tameka realized she'd hurt Lacey's feelings. "I'm sorry. I didn't mean—"

Lacey made an impatient gesture. "You have a right to your opinion."

But Tameka could tell Lacey was angry. Her

mouth was tight, her posture stiff. *Now Kyoto and Lacey are both mad at me,* Tameka thought with amazement. Being on people's bad sides was not something Tameka was familiar with. It made her more unhappy than ever.

★

By eight-thirty on Wednesday evening, Nicole figured she had procrastinated long enough. She wiped her sweaty palms on her shorts, picked up the phone, and dialed the number she'd written down on a little scrap of paper.

"Hello?"

"Hello. May I speak to Cole, please?" Nicole's heart was knocking.

"I'm Cole."

"Um, hi. This is Nicole Philips-Smith. Your band is supposed to play at my party Saturday night. . . ."

Cole didn't say anything, so Nicole nervously rushed on. "I just wanted to make sure you knew how to get to my house. And are you going to have a lot of equipment? We only have one plug in the backyard, and it—"

"This is Nicole?" Cole interrupted.

"Yeah. I'm the girl who's having the party."

"The party that was canceled, right?"

"Canceled?" Nicole squeaked. "Who told you that?"

"Lacey. She said someone on the team called this afternoon and told her—"

Nicole's blood suddenly ran cold. Sheila! Sheila had to be behind this. She'd started a rumor that Nicole's party was canceled. *Who else did she tell?* Nicole wondered frantically. *And why didn't they ask me about my party? Do they really trust Sheila?*

"Hello?" Cole was saying when Nicole tuned back in to their conversation. "Are you still there?"

"Yes, I'm here. And so's my party. I mean, my party *isn't* canceled. You've got to show up."

"Oh. Well, this is kind of a bummer. But we can't play for you now. I already told this chick Sheila that we'd play at *her* party that night."

"Oh. Right. Well, thanks anyway. Bye." Nicole turned off the phone and stood staring down at it. Sheila had tricked her again. And Nicole had absolutely no idea how to get *un*tricked.

She dialed Geena's number, but Mrs. Di Gregorio said Geena was already in bed. Nicole thanked her and hung up. It was eight-forty on a school night—too late to call everyone and tell them that the rumor was a lie.

I'll tell everyone tomorrow at practice, Nicole decided. But she knew two Stars who probably wouldn't care: Fiona and Lacey. If Cole and Josh's band was playing at Sheila's, that was where they'd be.

Nicole hated to admit it, but it was beginning to look as though Sheila would be choosing her clothes in the very near future.

CHAPTER 9

NICOLE DIDN'T SEE SHEILA UNTIL THE next day at school, during lunch. Sheila was sitting with Rory at a table near the windows. The girls had their heads together and were laughing about something.

Probably me, Nicole thought sourly. She tried to ignore them and pay attention to what Jordan was saying. Nicole had already told her and Rose that Sheila was spreading a rumor that her party was called off.

Nicole's eyes kept straying back to Sheila's laughing face. Finally she couldn't take it anymore. She tossed down her napkin and stood up. "I'll be right back," she told her friends.

"Nicole—don't go over there," Rose advised.

"Don't give her the satisfaction," Jordan said in her shy way.

Nicole shrugged and kept going.

Sheila and Rory stopped talking and watched as Nicole approached their table.

"I just wanted to tell you what I think of your plan to ruin my party," Nicole said with quiet fury. "I think only a total creep could think of something so low."

Sheila ran a hand through her silky hair and gave Nicole a mocking smile. "You look scared. I hate to see one of my teammates so unhappy. Tell you what. Why don't we call off our little bet? I think it's pretty clear who's going to win."

"*I'm* going to win," Nicole said furiously.

"You think?"

"I *know*."

"Then why don't we make the bet more interesting?" Sheila asked.

Nicole put one hand on her hip. "What do you have in mind?"

"Whoever loses quits the Stars."

Nicole swallowed hard. She didn't want to agree. But how could she say no? If she did, she'd have to endure a season of Sheila's smirks. And imagine what she'd get if she won . . . Sheila would be off the Stars forever.

"Whoever loses quits." Nicole stepped forward and stuck out her hand.

Sheila shook it eagerly.

★

Mr. Thomas motioned the team toward where he was standing on the sidelines. "Grab a drink of water and let's get organized for a scrimmage."

Tameka jogged up to the oversized water cooler Mrs. Essex had brought. Lacey and the rest of the team were right behind her. Tameka filled a paper cup to the very top with icy water. She backed up to make room for Lacey, accidentally splashing some water onto Lacey's cleat.

"Hey—watch it!" Lacey's tone made it clear she was still angry at Tameka.

"Sorry," Tameka said. She was wondering if she should apologize to Lacey for insulting Mrs. Essex, or give her friend more time to cool off. She'd already *had* two days.

"Yo, Tameka!"

Tameka looked up. Lacey was smirking at her. Then a splash of cold water hit Tameka right between the eyes. For a split second Tameka was angry, but then she realized the water felt incredibly refreshing.

"Thank you! Now take that!" Tameka yelled as she tossed the contents of her cup toward Lacey.

Lacey ducked—and the water hit Sheila and Geena instead.

"You missed me! You missed me!" Lacey sang out.

Tameka laughed, and the tension she'd been holding inside for the past few days lessened somewhat.

Sheila was holding a small bottle of carbonated water, which she shook up and aimed at Tameka. The water went everywhere—soaking Tameka, Tess, Yardley, Yasmine, and Fiona.

"Hey!" Fiona yelled, hiding behind Nicole.

Tameka, Yardley, and Tess ran for the cooler.

All this happened in a few seconds—about the amount of time it took Mrs. Essex to back out of the way.

Mr. Thomas wasn't as fast. He got splattered when Rory shook up *her* water and aimed it at Kyoto.

"That's enough!" Mr. Thomas hollered.

Yardley filled a cup and handed it to Tess.

Tess poured the water down Sheila's shirt.

Yardley handed the next cup to Tameka. Tameka began sneaking up on Lacey from behind.

"Tameka! Ann! Thomas!" Mr. Thomas bellowed. "I said, *that's enough!*"

Tameka froze.

The whole team was looking from Tameka to Mr. Thomas, who was standing with his hands on his hips. Tameka felt her anger mount. Why couldn't her dad let them have some fun? Why did he have to ruin everything? And why did he have to pick on her?

"Why are you yelling at me?" Tameka shouted.

"I just wanted—"

"You wanted to blame me for something I didn't even start!" Tameka's hands were clenched at her sides, and she was staring angrily at her father.

Mr. Thomas smiled as if this were all just some silly misunderstanding. "I didn't mean to single you out."

"So why did you?"

"I—"

"Forget it! I don't want to hear your excuses." Tameka stomped toward the parking lot and home.

"Meeki, come back!" Tess called.

Tameka didn't stop. So what if there were still fifteen minutes left in practice? She'd had enough.

"Hey, wait!" Tess jogged up to Tameka's side. "Are you okay?"

"No."

"Why not?"

"I hate having my dad as coach." *I wish he would quit*, she added to herself. *That way Marina would have to come back.*

Tameka heard her dad's car pull into the driveway. She ran to her room and closed the door. He'd want to give her a lecture about respecting him and honoring her commitment to soccer. She knew he'd be mad that she'd left practice early, and without permission.

But five minutes passed. Then half an hour. An hour. Mr. Thomas never knocked.

Now Tameka didn't know what to do. She was relieved, since she hated her dad's lectures. But she was also confused about why she'd been spared. And hungry. She wasn't sure what to do if her dad called her to dinner.

"Tameka!"

It was Kenya, Tameka's older sister, calling.

Tameka opened her door. "Yeah?"

"Phone for you."

Tameka picked up the phone in the hallway. "Hello?"

"Hi. It's Rose."

"Hey, Rose."

"I was just calling to wish you luck on Saturday."

Tameka's mom passed by and gently tapped her shoulder. "Dinner's ready," she whispered.

"Coming," Tameka told her mom. She'd decided to face her dad. She'd faint if she didn't eat something soon.

"Yeah, it's the first game of the season," Tameka said into the phone. "I wish you could be there to see it. Or better yet, to *play* in it."

"Me too. But orchestra practice starts at two-thirty."

"Well, I'll call you and let you know how we do," Tameka promised. She planned to make the game sound as exciting as possible. That way maybe Rose would realize that soccer was much cooler than orchestra.

After she'd hung up, Tameka went downstairs and sat at her usual spot at the table. Her dad was standing at the sink, peeling a mango. She didn't say anything to him.

Kenya and Mrs. Thomas chatted as they put the food on the table. Spicy black beans, yellow rice, grilled catfish, corn bread. And, apparently, sliced mango for dessert. Tameka's stomach rumbled.

"How was soccer practice today?" Mrs. Thomas asked as everyone settled in at the table.

"Awful." Tameka twirled her fork.

Tameka's mom shot a puzzled look at her dad.

Mr. Thomas sighed. "I was hoping you'd be over this little tantrum by now."

Tameka's anger flared the way a fire does when someone pours gas on it. "I haven't had a tantrum since I was five."

"So what do you call this?"

"Fury!" Tameka shouted. "The way you treated me today was so unfair." She turned to Kenya. "Everyone was having a water fight, but Dad only yelled at me. He totally singled me out, and I didn't even start it."

Kenya shrugged. "Parents do that kind of thing."

"See?" Mr. Thomas said. "Even your sister thinks you're overreacting."

Tameka's eyes were burning with angry tears as she stumbled to her feet. "Well, my sister doesn't know anything about it. She doesn't know that you let AYSO break up my team. Or that you didn't try to stop Marina from quitting. Or that you make me carry equipment while my friends play. It's not fair!"

Mr. Thomas just rubbed his eyes and sighed.

But Mrs. Thomas gave Tameka a no-nonsense look. "I never want to hear you speak to your father that way again," she told Tameka levelly. "You may go to your room now."

"But I'm hungry!"

"That doesn't give you the right to ruin our dinner. I'll bring you a tray after I've finished eating."

"Fine." Tameka left the kitchen with as much dignity as she could gather. Up in her room, she lay down on the bed and stared at the ceiling.

As she listened to the distant sounds of her family eating dinner, Tameka found herself getting more and more angry. Everything had gone wrong, and it was all her dad's fault.

If he hadn't agreed to coach the Stars, Marina would have been forced to stay.

And if he had encouraged her to be more serious about school, she would have ended up in the Gifted and Talented class with Tess.

Nicole and Geena spent Friday afternoon getting ready for Saturday's party. They swept and hosed down the patio, washed chairs, and decorated the backyard. Then they moved into the kitchen, where they mixed up a double batch of chocolate chip cookies.

All that time, Nicole was trying to think of the best way to tell Geena that her bet with Sheila had grown much more serious. She also needed to ask Geena a favor.

Nicole finally got up her nerve just as the first cookies were coming out of the oven and filling the kitchen with a delicious smell. "I don't know why we're going to all this trouble," she said. "Probably nobody will come to my party anyway."

"I'm coming."

"Name one other person you know who will definitely be here."

"Jordan. Rose. And you told me your friends Bridget and Laura promised to come."

"Yeah. Well, I meant Stars. Current Stars. I'm going to lose my bet unless they show up."

"At least everyone knows your party isn't canceled now. I can't believe Sheila pulled that stunt! Anyway, I guess we just have to wait and see what happens."

"Actually, I was thinking I might do more than just wait around."

"What do you mean?"

"Well, Sheila started a rumor about me. Why shouldn't I start one about her? I could say she's saying nasty things about the Stars."

Geena frowned. She continued to spoon batter onto the cookie sheet without commenting.

"I could say Sheila said Tess is bossy." Nicole helped herself to a finger of batter. "Or that Yasmine eats like a pig."

"How would Sheila know that?" Geena's tone was impatient.

"Um, I guess she wouldn't. But you don't have to say that. You could pretend Sheila said whatever you want."

"*I* could?"

"Yeah. See, I figure the Stars won't believe anything *I* say about Sheila. They know we're enemies. So I want you to spread the rumors."

"Nicole, you're incredible. How do you come up with this stuff? Do you have some sort of nasty behavior textbook? Or have you been watching the soaps again?"

"I just want to give Sheila a taste of her own medicine."

"Well, have fun."

"What does that mean?"

"That means I'm not going to help. If you want to spread rumors about Sheila, do the dirty work yourself. Personally, I think you're going too far just to avoid wearing a stupid outfit to school one day."

"That's not the bet anymore."

Geena looked up from her work. "It isn't?"

"No. Now whoever loses has to drop off the team."

"Nicole! How could you make a bet like that?"

Geena didn't seem worried, the way Nicole had hoped she would. Instead she looked angry.

"What happens if you lose?" Geena demanded.

"I'm not planning to lose."

"I'm sure Sheila isn't either!"

Nicole knew that. But she was trying not to think about losing. The idea of having to quit soccer was just too awful.

The Stars' first game of the season was against the Satellites.

When Tameka got to the field on Saturday, she immediately looked for Sarah. She spotted the tall girl standing with some of her new teammates on the opposite sidelines.

"Hey, Sarah!"

Sarah looked up, smiled, waved, ran over, and gave Tameka a hug. Tess and Yasmine came up, so Sarah hugged them too. "This is so weird," Sarah said. "I can't believe I'm going to be playing *against* you guys."

"How are things on the Satellites?" Tess asked.

Sarah shook her head and rolled her eyes. But she looked amused. "So not the Stars! Mindy, our coach, makes us do everything ourselves. We have to take turns leading warm-ups, and last week *I* had to run a dribbling drill."

"You?" Tess snorted with laughter.

"Tess!" Tameka said.

"No, it's okay," Sarah said with an amused shake of her head. "It *was* funny. I mean, I'm the world's worst dribbler. But my drill actually went okay."

"Girls!" Mr. Thomas called. "Let's talk about the lineup!"

Sarah made a face. "Speaking of lineups—we have to create our own. It took us about two hours to fight it out. Everyone wanted to be in the midfield. Anyway, see you out there."

"Bye."

Sarah ran back across the field, and Tameka grudgingly followed Tess and Yasmine to where the Stars were gathering. "Mindy sounds nice," she remarked. "I mean, Dad never lets us run drills."

"I was on a team like that once," Yasmine said. "Everyone was always fighting. And I got stuck in the goal for about half the games."

"Nice shirt!" Geena told Mr. Thomas.

Mr. Thomas beamed. His T-shirt was the same yellow as the Stars' jerseys, and it said COACH in bold black letters. "Do you like it? My family gave it to me."

"Mom did," Tameka corrected him.

"Right." Mr. Thomas frowned and cleared his throat. "Well, before I give you your positions, Tess reminded me to tell the new players about short-sided games."

"I already know about them," Kyoto said. "We played short-sided on my team in California too."

"Well, then, explain it to *me*," Yardley said.

Mr. Thomas nodded at Kyoto.

"With a traditional team you have eleven players on the field at once," Kyoto told her. "Short-sided, it's fewer."

"We can have a max of nine players on the field," Mr. Thomas added. "Two of you sit out."

"Who gets to sit out?" Yardley asked.

Gets to? Tameka slid a look at Yasmine. "Yard sounds like she's dying to play," she whispered.

"Probably nervous," Yasmine whispered back.

"I'll rotate you," Mr. Thomas was saying. "Over the season, everyone will get an equal amount of time on the field." He glanced at a diagram he had attached to his clipboard. "Kyoto, will you please play goalkeeper?"

"Sure!" Kyoto pawed through the equipment bag and pulled out the multicolored goalkeeper's jersey. She pulled it over her head.

"Sheila, I'd like you to play left defender," Mr. Thomas went on. "Nicole, right defender."

Tameka gave Nicole a sympathetic look. She knew Nicole liked to stay as far away from Sheila as possible.

"Lacey, left midfielder," Mr. Thomas continued. "Fiona, center midfield. Geena, right midfield."

Tess sent Tameka a smile. Tameka knew why she was happy: It was beginning to look as if they'd both end up on the front line, which was exactly where Tess liked to be.

Tameka smiled back. She and Tess were an unstoppable attacking machine. And it would be nice to start the season scoring a goal together.

"Tess, right wing," Mr. Thomas continued.

"Yes!" Tess exclaimed.

Mr. Thomas glanced up, smiled at her, and then went on. "Yasmine, left wing. And Yardley, you'll be center attacker and our team captain for the day."

Yardley's jaw dropped. "Team captain?" she spluttered. "But—I don't know what to do!"

Tess draped an arm across Yardley's shoulders.

"It's not hard," she said soothingly. "All you have to do is represent the team during the coin toss. And I'll help you during the game."

Tameka glared at her dad. How could he leave her on the bench during the first game of the season? Mr. Thomas didn't seem to notice her angry look. He was scribbling something on his board and humming to himself.

"Captains on the field!" the ref hollered.

"Oh no." Yardley looked scared.

Tess gave her a pat on the back. "Don't worry. The ref will tell you what to do."

Yardley clumsily jogged off.

Tameka sank down on the team's aluminum bench and crossed her arms. She stuck out her lip in a furious pout.

Yasmine gave her a surprised look. "Something wrong?"

"I'm benched!"

"Well, someone has to be."

"Yeah. But it doesn't have to be me. Or maybe it does! And you know why? Because my dad doesn't want it to look as if he's favoring his daughter by actually letting her play!"

Mr. Thomas overheard. In fact, most of the

Stars were staring at Tameka with amazement. She knew they were probably shocked she was making such a fuss. Well, too bad. She felt like fussing.

"Tameka, may I have a word with you?" Mr. Thomas asked.

"No, you may not." She twisted around on the bench so that she was facing away from her dad.

"Let's line it up!" the ref called.

"Have fun out there," Mr. Thomas told the team.

Tess and Yasmine hesitated as the other girls jogged onto the field.

"You okay?" Tess asked.

Tameka shrugged. "Go play."

"Come on." Yasmine pulled Tess onto the field. She gave Tameka a backward glance. "Cheer for us."

Tameka made a face. She wasn't in the mood to cheer. She was in the mood to stomp her feet and whine. She didn't *want* to sit on the bench and watch Tess play with Yardley.

The teams got into position. Sarah was playing defender for the Satellites.

Yardley, Tess, and Yasmine lined up around the ball. The ref blew her whistle. Yardley immediately kicked the ball as hard as she could into Satellite territory.

Tameka sat up straighter. What did Yard think she was doing?

On the bench next to her, Rory dropped her head. "This girl is a disaster," she muttered.

The most important thing on a kickoff was keeping control of the ball. Instead, Yard had just handed control to the Satellites.

"It's Yard's first season," Mr. Thomas reminded them. "Probably she thought that was a good way to get the ball closer to the goal."

"Or maybe she thinks she's playing football," Rory said with a sad laugh.

"We'll have to practice kickoffs next week." Mr. Thomas wrote something down on his clipboard.

Meanwhile, Tess and Yasmine were dashing forward in a mad attempt to get the ball back.

A Satellite midfielder wearing a red bandanna around her neck trapped the ball with her chest and let it drop to the ground. Then she dribbled diagonally for a few feet and passed outside. A Satellite attacker took the ball up the touchline.

Just as Fiona and Lacey were ganging up on her, the attacker gave the ball a hard boot into the center of the field. It landed in front of the Satellite center, who was wide open. She controlled the ball and began bolting toward the Stars' goal area.

"Be alert, Kyoto!" Mr. Thomas called.

"Stop her, Sheila!" Rory put in.

Tameka stayed silent.

Sheila and Nicole were pounding toward the Satellite attacker from opposite directions. When they got close, the Satellite tapped the ball to her left wing.

Nicole put on the brakes and changed direction, running after the ball.

Before she could get to it, the wing caught the pass and shot. The ball zipped along the ground, hit the Stars' left goalpost, and bounced in over Kyoto's head.

"Goal—Satellites!"

Rory gave Tameka a wry look. "Nice start to the season."

Tameka shrugged. She didn't know what to feel. Angry that the Satellites had scored? Or happy that Yardley had messed up?

chapter 11

TESS HAD A WHISPERED CONFERENCE with Yardley as the teams moved back into position. On the second kickoff Yardley passed Tess the ball like a good center. Tess dribbled up the right touchline, moving fast. A Satellite attacker was right on her heels. And so was Yardley!

Tameka could see Tess yelling and motioning Yardley back. The Satellite tried to take advantage of the confusion and steal the ball. Yardley backpedaled a few steps and fell. Tess went down on her knees. The ball bounced out of bounds.

"Throw-in—Satellites!"

"Beautiful play," Rory said with a giggle.

Things didn't improve much in the next ten

minutes. Yardley did her best to stick with the ball, no matter where it was on the field or who had possession. Her clumsiness seemed to be contagious. The Stars were tripping all over the place. Fortunately, Kyoto made several great saves. But about six minutes after their first goal, one of the Satellite wings fired a shot in over her head.

"Take two!" the ref said, calling for the substitution break. The Satellites led 2 to 0.

Tameka retied her shoelaces and stood up to stretch. She was ready to play.

Mr. Thomas smiled as the team gathered around. "That was a bit of a rocky start," he admitted. "But the first game is bound to be rough."

Tameka glanced at Tess. Her face was red from exertion—and probably fury.

Mr. Thomas turned to Yardley. "Yard, you need to think about staying in position. When you're playing on the front line, your job is to attack. Let the midfielders and defenders do their work when the ball is on our side of the field. They need someone to pass to, so stay out of the way."

Yardley nodded thoughtfully, as if the idea of staying in position was completely new to her.

"Dad," Tameka said. "We're running out of time. Substitutions, remember?"

"I remember. Rory, go in for Geena."

The ref tooted her whistle.

"That's it?" Tameka demanded.

"That's it. I'll put you in after the half."

Tess shot Tameka an I-can't-believe-this look, took a deep breath, and headed out toward the halfway line.

"How could you leave Yardley in?" Tameka demanded of her father. "She's the worst!"

"And she's not going to get any better sitting on the sidelines," Mr. Thomas said mildly. "I wanted to give her an opportunity to apply what I've just told her."

Tameka groaned in frustration. Her father was going to make her spend the entire first half of the first game on the sidelines. Talk about unfair!

★

Yardley was better in the second fifteen minutes of the game. Not that she made any great plays, but at least she stayed out of Tess's and Yasmine's way.

About five minutes after the substitution break, Rory took possession of the ball off a Satellite throw-in. She dribbled aggressively into Satellite territory, quick-footing it around a Satellite midfielder. Glancing up, she got a long pass off to Yasmine.

Yasmine sped toward the ball but slipped. Before Yaz could get to her feet, Sarah intercepted. She looked up to read the field. Fiona was coming at her like a speeding locomotive, so Sarah passed—directly to Tess.

"Oh. Oops!" Sarah yelled. "I didn't mean to do that."

Tess trapped the ball and in one fluid move sent it toward the Satellites' goal—a powerful ground ball. The sleepy Satellite goalkeeper missed it.

"Goal—Stars!"

Geena was laughing. "Sarah forgot what team she's on!"

Out on the field, Tess was patting Sarah on the back. Everyone was laughing. The Satellites didn't seem too upset about Sarah's blunder. After all, they were still ahead.

The Satellites took the kickoff. They were just mounting an attack on the Stars' goal when the half ended.

Tameka didn't enjoy halftime much. She felt

out of synch with her teammates. They were all keyed up, chattering about the first half. Lacey and Yasmine were laughing about Sarah's pass. Nicole and Geena were telling Kyoto what an incredible goalkeeper she was. Everyone was downing cups of water and munching on orange slices.

On the opposite sidelines, Tameka could see Sarah standing with some of her new teammates. She hated how easily everyone was adjusting to their new teams. Didn't they miss the old Stars?

And where was Marina? Tameka scanned the little crowd of parents and fans. Marina wasn't there. Tameka knew she hadn't promised to come to *all* the games, but she hadn't thought she'd miss the *first* one.

"Want some oranges?" Tess asked Tameka.

"No. I'm not hungry. I haven't even played yet."

Tess smiled. "I can't believe you're so mad. You're the one who taught me that everyone deserves a chance to play."

"Yeah—including me! Can't you see how unfair Dad is being? Would he make a player who wasn't his daughter sit out an entire half?"

Tess sighed. "I don't know. But it's over now. I'm sure he'll play you in the second half."

"He'd better."

★

It's now or never, Nicole told herself. She knew she had to get started spreading rumors about Sheila, but where to begin?

Tameka looked stormy—better not to bother her. Tess and Rory were lost causes. Ditto Fiona and Lacey. Nicole's gaze fell on Yardley. Perfect!

Nicole walked to where Yardley was sitting in the grass, retying her cleats.

Yardley smiled as Nicole sat down next to her. "How's it going?"

"Not that good." Nicole did her best to look sad. "I can't believe what I just heard. Sheila says it's your fault we're losing the game. She says you should be yanked off the front line."

Yardley studied Nicole as if she were some mold in a petri dish. Her expression was hard to read. "Sheila told you that?" Yardley asked.

"Yeah."

"I though you two hated each other."

"Well, I kind of overheard Sheila. She was actually talking to Rory."

"May I ask you a question?"

Nicole shifted nervously and began to pluck up grass. "Sure—what?"

"Let's assume Sheila actually did say something nasty about me. . . ."

"She did!"

"Okay, then tell me what possible motivation you have to repeat what she said. Are you trying to hurt my feelings?"

"No! I just . . . thought you should know what kind of person she is."

Yardley got up and brushed the grass clippings off her shorts. "Thanks. I've learned a lot about *both* of you."

Nicole flopped back in the grass and covered her eyes with her hands. Whoa! Talk about a major backfire!

★

Mr. Thomas gathered the Stars together so that he could announce the lineup for the second half. Tameka stood next to Tess, staring at her cleats. She was so furious with her dad that she couldn't make herself look at him.

"All right, everyone," Mr. Thomas said. "You pulled things together nicely in that second fifteen minutes of play. I can tell you're really beginning to think like a team."

He was right, and that made Tameka feel even more miserable. Yaz was standing with Yard. And Geena was braiding Kyoto's hair. Most of the Stars still weren't being very nice to Rory and Sheila. But half the new team members already seemed part of the group.

"Geena, I'd like you to go in for Lacey," Mr. Thomas continued. "And Tameka, you can take over for Nicole as right defender."

Defender? Dad makes me wait an entire half to play—and then he puts me in as defender? Tameka had been envisioning herself on the front line, helping Yaz and Tess tie up the score.

"Dad!" Tameka complained. "I don't want to play defense."

She saw Tess and Yaz exchange surprised looks. The rest of the team was watching too.

Mr. Thomas gave Tameka a fed-up look. "Well, better luck next Saturday."

"I don't want to wait until next Saturday!"

"What do you plan to do instead?" Mr. Thomas didn't look sympathetic. Clearly, he wasn't going to switch Tameka's position without a fight.

Tameka felt something in her snap. "If you won't let me play on the front line, I'm not playing at all!"

"Give me a break," Sheila muttered.

Tameka knew her teammates must think she was acting ridiculous. But she couldn't stop herself.

"Fine," Mr. Thomas said tightly. "Nicole, stay in."

"She can have my position," Yardley said meekly.

"No."

Kyoto was staring at Tameka. "What's your problem?"

"It's none of your business."

"Are you still mad your old team got split up?" Kyoto's tone was mocking.

"Maybe. So?"

"That is so lame. Do you think AYSO makes up these rules just to make you unhappy?"

"No!"

"Because they don't. They do it because they think it's best for everyone to play on balanced teams. Why don't you stop thinking about how great last season was and start trying to make this season better?"

The ref blew her whistle. "Let's line it up!"

Kyoto turned on her heel and stomped toward the goal area. Most of the rest of the team moved off. But Tess, Yasmine, and Nicole hesitated. Lacey, who was on the bench, was listening in.

"Tameka," Nicole said uneasily. "Why don't you play?"

"I'm not in the mood."

"Well, get in the mood!" Tess's tone was less kind. "You're acting completely immature. Sheila and Rory are making themselves part of this team. What's your hang-up?"

"Maybe I want to play for a coach who treats people fairly."

"Are you people playing?" the ref called.

"Come on," Tess said angrily. "If Tameka wants

to pout, let her." Tess, Yaz, and Nicole trotted onto the field. Lacey sat down on the bench and silently drew her feet up under her.

Tameka didn't expect any sympathy from Lacey. Lacey had been mad at her ever since she'd invited Marina to practice. Tameka suddenly felt worn out. She used to be the one who kept peace on the Stars. Now she was suddenly the team troublemaker.

chapter 12

THE SECOND HALF WAS PRETTY MUCH A repeat of the first. Tameka watched in grim silence as the Satellites continued to test the Stars' defense. Kyoto, Sheila, and Nicole did a good job of keeping the ball out of the Stars' goal. Yaz, Tess, and the midfielders worked hard. But they couldn't score without some help in the center—and Yardley wasn't offering any.

When the ref signaled the end of the game, the score was 1 to 3. The Stars lined up to shake hands with the Satellites. Lacey ran out on the field to join the line.

Tameka didn't. Why should she shake hands with girls she hadn't even played against?

Mrs. Essex and Mr. Thomas clapped for the team as they straggled off the field.

Fiona flopped down in the grass. "I bet I ran four miles during that game. I'm beat."

"Get up." Lacey offered her a hand. "You'll start sneezing."

Fiona was allergic to . . . well, basically everything outside. Tameka knew she wasn't supposed to get too close to grass.

"I don't care," Fiona said. "I'm too tired to move."

"Too tired to move—to Regina's?" Mrs. Essex asked.

Fiona immediately sat up and jumped to her feet. "For that, I can move."

"Who's coming?" Lacey asked.

"The whole team," Mrs. Essex said.

Regina's was a fabulous pizza place down by the lake. They had about fifty different toppings—including pineapple. Tameka was eating her way down the list alphabetically. She'd already tried basil leaves, barbecued chicken, and bean sprouts. Bell peppers were next.

Yaz nudged Tameka. "Can I get a ride with you?"

Tameka made a face. "This is such a rip-off. Marina used to take us out for ice cream. So now Dad and Mrs. Essex are going to take us out for pizza. I think it's dumb."

"Pizza is never dumb," Yasmine argued.

"Who needs a ride?" Mr. Thomas asked. "We have room for three."

"Make that four," Tameka said. "I'm not coming."

"Suit yourself." Mr. Thomas shrugged.

But Mrs. Essex gave her a pleading look. "Sweetie, come on. Haven't we had enough unhappiness for one day?"

Tameka wanted to join her teammates. Being angry all the time was a lot of work. But she couldn't let her dad off that easy. "I'm not coming," she repeated firmly.

"Want me to drop you home?" Mr. Thomas asked.

"No thanks. I'll walk."

Without saying goodbye to anyone, Tameka headed across the field. Nobody stopped her. Nobody called after her. Well, so what? Getting away from the other girls felt good. Tameka could sense that they didn't like the way she was acting.

Walking felt good, too. It suited Tameka's stormy mood. And she had plenty of energy after sitting out the entire game.

At Regina's, Nicole got herself a mushroom slice and then chose a seat between Geena and Yasmine. She didn't really feel like eating, but she didn't want to go home either. She wanted to savor her last day of being a Star. As soon as Sheila's party started that evening, she'd have to quit the team.

Nicole was resigned to the fact that she was going to lose the bet. If her plan to spread nasty rumors about Sheila had succeeded, she *might* have had a fighting chance. But her plan had bombed. All she'd succeeded in doing was making Yardley mad at her. Which just made it all the more likely she'd lose.

"Don't eat too much!" Sheila called out to the table. "We have piles of food at my house."

Geena glanced at Nicole to see how she'd react. Nicole just slipped farther down in her seat.

"Let's get another soda." Geena grabbed Nicole's arm and pulled her toward the line. "What's going on?"

"*Nothing* is going on. Everyone's going to Sheila's tonight. I lost."

Geena thought for a second. "Listen, why don't you tell Sheila that?"

"Why? So she can laugh in my face?"

"No, so you can stop this silly bet. I don't want you off the Stars. I'd miss you."

Nicole gave Geena a weary smile. "I don't want to quit."

"So ask Sheila to call off the bet. Maybe she'll surprise you."

"I don't know . . ."

"I'll go get her," Geena offered. "Wait here."

Before Nicole could protest, Geena hurried off toward the table. A moment later Nicole watched Sheila approach. For once, Rory wasn't with her.

"Geena said you wanted to talk to me." Sheila's tone was cool.

Nicole took a deep breath. She glanced over her shoulder. The ordering line was only a few feet away. She wanted to be sure none of the Stars would overhear what she had to say. For now the coast was clear. She didn't see any yellow jerseys in line.

"Yeah. I, um, I want to call off our bet."

"Why?"

"Because I know I'm going to lose."

Sheila threw back her head and let out a long, delighted laugh.

Nicole clenched her hands and fought to control her temper. "Listen, Sheila, I'll be happy to wear whatever stupid outfit you pick out for me. But I don't want to drop out of the Stars. I love this team—even with you on it."

"So sweet. So sad." Sheila shook her head and gave Nicole a mocking look. "But, Miss Country Day Council President, I guess you should have thought about that *before* you made the bet. I'm not letting you off the hook now."

Sheila spun around and practically danced over to the table. Nicole was stunned. No more Stars? She walked back to her seat in a daze.

"How did it go?" Geena whispered.

"She laughed in my face."

"What are you going to do now?"

"Have a Goodbye, Stars party. And hope for a miracle."

★

When Tameka got to the end of her street, she kept walking. She knew her mother would be surprised if she came home now. She'd ask all sorts of questions that Tameka didn't want to answer.

Tameka walked on into downtown Beachside. As she passed the big brick music hall, she heard distant music and thought of Rose. Could that sound be the youth orchestra rehearsing?

On impulse, she walked up the sweeping stone steps and tried the main door. It wasn't locked, so she walked into the lobby. The music was louder now. Tameka opened another door and found herself in a large auditorium with row after row of plush seats and an enormous glass chandelier. She vaguely remembered coming here for a performance of *Peter and the Wolf* when she was in elementary school.

A large orchestra was set up on the stage. The conductor, a balding man wearing black pants and a white shirt, had his back to the auditorium. His arms were outstretched, and he bounced in time with the music. A few people were scattered throughout the seats. Probably parents.

Tameka slipped into a seat near the back. There was Rose, sitting behind a black music stand at the front of the stage. She was sawing away on her violin. The music swelled. Rose and the other violinists played even faster—and then suddenly the music stopped.

After a brief pause, the conductor began telling the orchestra something Tameka couldn't hear. When he was finished talking, the group broke up and began putting their instruments away. Once they'd packed up, they came down the stage steps into the audience. Tameka managed to intercept Rose as she headed up the red-carpeted aisle.

"Tameka!" Rose did a double take. "What are you doing here?"

"I just heard the end of your rehearsal. Not bad."

"Thanks. But why aren't you out celebrating with the team?"

"I'm sick of the team."

"But you just had your first game!"

"I know."

"Come on," Rose said warmly. "Walk me to my bus stop and tell me what's going on."

The girls headed outside and up the street. Tameka told Rose about fighting with her dad and Kyoto. Rose listened carefully without commenting. She bounced her violin case against her leg as she walked.

"See?" Tameka finished. "The team hasn't been the same since you left."

Rose laughed.

"What's so funny?"

"Well, to me, it doesn't sound as if the Stars have changed much. We did plenty of fighting last season too."

"How come it seems worse now?"

"Because you used to keep the peace," Rose said gently. "If anything major about the Stars has changed, it's you."

Tameka let that sink in for a moment. She *had* changed a lot since the previous season. Going to soccer camp had changed her. Finding out that her school thought she was stupid and inept had changed her. And having her dad for a coach had changed her too.

Maybe getting the old Stars back really was impossible.

chapter 13

TAMEKA WALKED UP HER DRIVEWAY JUST as her dad was pulling in. She waited while he got out of the car.

"Where have you been?" Mr. Thomas's tone was sad, weary, resigned.

"Walking."

Mr. Thomas waited—obviously hoping for a more complete explanation.

"I found Rose and we had a long talk."

"A long talk. I think that's exactly what we need too." Mr. Thomas motioned for Tameka to join him on the front steps.

Tameka sat down on the scratchy concrete. She stared out at the street and prepared herself for a lecture. She knew exactly what she'd hear. That she'd been disrespectful to her dad and to the Stars by not playing that afternoon. That temper tantrums were fine when you were six, but not when you were twelve. That it was time for her to grow up and accept the team the way it was.

Mr. Thomas sat down, resting his big hands on his knees. He took a deep breath and seemed to gather his thoughts. "Tameka, do you know why I'm coaching the Stars?"

Tameka shrugged one shoulder. "Because Marina quit."

Mr. Thomas laughed and shook his head. "No."

"Then why?"

"Sweetie, I started coaching the Stars so that we could spend some time together, get to know each other better. You may not realize it yet, but the next few years are going to be rough ones for you. I've already had one daughter become a teenager, and I know what I'm talking about."

"Kenya *has* been a pain the past few years."

"Let's not drag your sister into this," Mr. Thomas said. "The point is, I want you and me to be friends. I thought this would help."

Tameka glanced up at her dad, her throat tightening. She could hear the hurt in his voice, and it made her feel *this* big. "Daddy—"

Mr. Thomas held up one hand. "Let me finish. I can see that my little experiment flopped. Spending all this quality time together is hurting our relationship more than helping it. So I spoke to Larissa. She's willing to handle the team without me."

"You're quitting?" Tameka asked.

"Bingo."

"Dad, don't quit. You're a great coach."

"That doesn't mean I'm a good coach for *you*. I've seen how unhappy you've been ever since soccer started back up."

"Yeah. But soccer's only part of it."

"What's the other part?"

Tameka studied her father's face. She could tell he really wanted to know what was bothering her. So she told him something she hadn't told anyone else. "It's school. Ever since Tess got into that Gifted and Talented class I've been feeling dumb. I mean, I know I'm not. But, well, maybe I am and I didn't realize it."

"You're not."

"Well then, how come they put Tess in that class and not me? I know as much math as she does!"

"What's your theory?"

"Oh, it's probably because she's such an incredible go-getter. She always wants to be the best."

"Don't you want to be the best?"

"Sometimes. But sometimes I get lazy."

"Maybe if you change your attitude this year, they'll let you into the Gifted and Talented class next year."

"I'd probably have to get straight A's."

"I think you can do that."

Tameka smiled. She thought so too. "And I think you can be a straight-A coach."

"As good as Marina?"

"Well . . ." Tameka laughed. "Marina's impossible to replace. But *someone* has to take over. And I like the idea of its being you."

Mr. Thomas gave her a sideways hug. "Then I'll stay."

Tameka put an arm around her dad and squeezed back. "Thanks."

★

After her dad went inside, Tameka walked over to Tess's house and knocked on the back screen door.

Tess appeared in the kitchen. Her face lit up when she saw Tameka standing there. "Hi! I've been meaning to call you all afternoon. But my phone's been ringing off the hook about tonight." She unlocked the door and pushed it open so that Tameka could come in.

Tameka shook her head as she stepped inside. "I'm sorry I was so weird today. Dad and I talked. I'm feeling much more normal now."

"Sure?"

"Positive. Dad and I agreed to start over. And I'm planning to do the same with Lacey and Kyoto . . . and Yardley. I'm sorry I yelled at you for liking her."

"I'm sorry I yelled at you for not playing."

Tameka smiled. "Truce?"

"Absolutely. But I totally wish you'd been at Regina's this afternoon. Yardley and I overheard this unbelievable conversation between Sheila and Nicole. We're pretty sure they have some sort of bet going. We think that whoever loses has to drop off the Stars."

"That's stupid!"

"I know." Tess sat down at the kitchen table with a sigh. "Yardley thinks the bet is related to the parties."

Tameka nodded slowly as she pulled out a chair and sat down. She'd been so distracted by her own problems for the past few weeks that she hadn't paid much attention to Nicole and Sheila. But now that she thought about it, something about their behavior did seem off.

"The way they both decided to have parties on the same night is strange," she said.

"Right," Tess agreed. "And Nicole's party was canceled, and then uncanceled. And Cole's band was playing at Nicole's and then suddenly switched to Sheila's. We think they're competing to see who can have the most popular party."

"So what are we going to do?"

"Nobody can decide! I've been on the phone with Yaz, Fiona, Lacey, Kyoto, and Yard all afternoon. Most everyone wants to go to Nicole's. And if I had to choose between having Sheila on the team and having Nicole on the team, I guess I'd pick Nicole. But still . . . I don't think losing either of them is right."

"I agree."

"So what should we do?"

"Give me a minute to think. . . ."

★

"Where *is* everyone?" Nicole was so nervous that she felt sick to her stomach. Sitting still was impossible. She walked back and forth in front of the windows in her room. She peered out at the street. No cars.

Geena glanced at her watch. "It's only seven-twenty-eight. The party isn't supposed to start for another two minutes."

Nicole glanced toward the window again. "Did you hear a car?"

"No! Come on, try to relax."

"How can I relax? If none of the Stars show up, I'm off the team. Not to mention the fact that I'll have to wear something hideous to school on Tuesday. I can just *imagine* what Sheila will think up!" Nicole saw herself wearing a babydoll dress and carrying a huge pacifier. That was the kind of thing Sheila thought was funny.

Nicole crossed to her full-length mirror and studied her reflection without really seeing it. "Do I look okay? Is this shirt lame?"

"Yes."

"Yes, it's lame?"

"No. Yes, you look okay!"

Both girls jumped when the doorbell rang.

"Someone's here!" Nicole said, grabbing Geena's hand. "I *told* you I heard a car."

They pounded down the stairs together. Nicole grabbed the doorknob, then rested her cheek against the door without opening it. "Please let it be a Star," she prayed.

Geena groaned. "Even if it is, she might leave before you let her in!"

Nicole stepped back and threw open the door. She almost fainted when she saw Tess, Tameka, and Yasmine standing on the stoop. Behind them were Kyoto and Yardley. Fiona, Lacey, Cole, Josh, and a couple of boys Nicole didn't know were standing on the grass surrounded by guitar cases, amplifiers, and coils of wire. Nicole was so surprised that she just stared at the group without speaking.

"Did you all come together?" Geena sounded stunned.

"Yes," Tameka said. "We know about the bet."

Nicole's brain clicked back into gear. "How?" she asked.

"It didn't take a genius to figure it out." Tameka laughed. "Well, maybe it did. Yardley did most of the figuring."

Suddenly Nicole began to realize what was happening. *Eight* of the Stars had come to her party. She'd won!

"You guys knew about the bet—and you decided to come here?" Nicole's throat was tight with emotion. "Does that mean you all want me to stay on the team?"

"Absolutely."

The incredible pressure Nicole had been feeling for the past few weeks blew away. She felt like dancing, or singing, or spinning in circles.

"Thanks! That's so sweet." Nicole went out onto the step and gave Tameka a long, relieved hug. "Come on in," she said, stepping back. "There's tons of food out back . . ."

Nicole let her voice trail off when she realized nobody was moving. Alarm bells started to go off in her mind.

"What's the matter?" she asked.

"We have a request before we come in."

"What?" Nicole asked fearfully.

"Well, if we come in and help you win the bet,

you can't make Sheila drop off the team. We want you to tell her the bet is off."

Nicole frowned. "What if I say no?"

Tameka shrugged. "Then we're heading over to Sheila's and making her the same offer."

"You can't win unless you agree to do what we want," Tess added.

Geena smiled, then laughed out loud. "Nicole, I think this is an offer you *can't* refuse."

Nicole didn't feel like dancing anymore. She wanted Sheila off the team. How could her teammates take that pleasure away from her? But then she remembered how miserable she'd been for the past few days, worrying that she was going to lose the Stars. Was is so crazy to think Sheila felt the same way?

"Well . . . okay," Nicole said reluctantly. "I'll tell Sheila the bet is off."

"Good!" Tameka smiled. "We actually didn't have a ride over to Sheila's. I don't know what we would have done if you'd refused!"

Nicole laughed halfheartedly. She showed everyone into the backyard and found a place for Cole and the band to set up. Then Tess, Tameka, and Yasmine pushed her toward the house.

"Go call Sheila," Fiona said.

"Get it over with," Kyoto added. "Then we can boogie down!"

Nicole groaned. "Oh, all right. Geena, can you come with me for moral support?"

"No problem."

The two girls trooped into the house, and Nicole dialed Sheila's number.

"Hello?" Sheila's voice was wary—as if she knew she was about to get bad news.

"I won!" Nicole crowed. "All the Stars are here."

"Nicole, you promised!" Geena said sharply.

"But, um, I have something to tell you—" Nicole added.

"No," Sheila interrupted. "I have something to tell *you*."

"What?"

"I'm not dropping off the team."

Nicole raised her eyebrows at Geena, who was listening curiously. "You're not?"

"No way. And I'm not wearing some stupid outfit to school, either. If you tell anyone I promised to, I'll say you're a liar."

"Oh." Under the circumstances, Nicole didn't

see any reason to tell Sheila what the Stars had done to keep her on the team. She figured Sheila had lost her right to know when she'd announced she was going to cheat on the bet.

"You may not like it," Sheila continued. "But the Stars are *my* team now too. You can't get rid of me just because you don't like me."

"Well, you can't get rid of me, either!" Nicole hung up quickly, before Sheila could reply.

"What was that all about?" Geena asked.

Nicole smiled. "Sheila wasn't interested in making peace."

"Does she want to stay on the Stars?"

"She *insists* on staying."

Geena rolled her eyes. "This team is crazy."

"True," Nicole said. "But it's ours. Come on, let's go join the party."

Soccer Tips from AYSO

WARMING UP

Warming up is essential to getting your heart, lungs, and muscles ready for a hard workout or practice. Warming up your body makes you more flexible and reduces the possibility of getting hurt. If you jump into practice without warming up, your muscles are tight and unprepared for the stress of activity. But gently warming up gets your body ready to play hard with less risk of injury.

Before practice, you should warm up for at least ten minutes. The ideal warm-up has three parts: Walking to get your blood flowing, stretching to get your muscles ready, and running to get your heart ready.

First, do a fast walk around the field. This gets the blood flowing through your whole body and tells your muscles to loosen up so that you're ready for stretching.

Stretching reduces muscle tension and gets the blood flowing freely in parts of your body that will come under heavy fire during your workout. You should concentrate on stretching your thighs, calves, lower back, groin, and gluteus maximus (a.k.a. your rear end). Stretch each muscle by flexing it tightly and then gently relaxing it. Never bounce through a stretch; rather, gently allow the muscle to stretch and then relax.

Some stretches to try:

- Sit on the ground and spread your legs. Lean over each thigh and feel the pull. Remember—don't bounce!
- While sitting, pull your feet together so that the bottoms of your shoes are touching and your feet are close to your body. Then gently push your knees to the ground.
- While standing, roll your arms in giant circles, first forward, then backward. Then gently rock your head from left to right.
- Place your hands on your waist, keep your feet shoulder width apart, and bend gently to the right. Feel the muscles stretch. Then pull your left arm over your head and feel the stretch increase. Repeat the exercise on the other side. After you've stretched out, get your heart moving by taking a brief jog or doing a few sprint-walk-sprint drills. Ask your coach which she prefers, but make sure stretching is a part of your—and your team's—practice routine.

After a workout, you should always cool down. Walk around until your heartbeat slows. Then repeat the stretches you did for your warm-up. You'll notice that your muscles are more flexible at the end of your workout and you can stretch easily. Your muscles will like the relief and will be in better shape for the next practice if you make sure to take care of them with proper stretching.

AYSO Soccer Definitions

Attacker: The player in control of the ball, attempting to score a goal. Attackers need speed, power, good ball control, and accurate aim. Sometimes referred to as forward.

AYSO: American Youth Soccer Organization, a nationwide organization guided by five principles:

1. Everyone plays
2. Balanced teams
3. Open registration
4. Positive coaching
5. Good sportsmanship

Cleats: Projections on the soles of soccer shoes that provide support and a better grip on the soccer field.

Defender: The player whose primary duty is to prevent the opposing team from getting a good shot at the goal. Defenders need sufficient speed to cover opposing players, good tackling skills, and determination to win control of the ball.

Dribbling: Moving the ball along the ground by a series of short taps with one or both feet.

Goal: Scored when the entire ball crosses the line between the goalposts and underneath the crossbar.

Goalkeeper: The last line of defense. The

goalkeeper is the only player who can use her hands during play within the penalty area.

Halftime: A five- to ten-minute break in the middle of a game.

Halfway line: A line that marks the middle of the field.

Midfielder: The player who supports the attack on the goal with accurate passes and hustles to get back to help the defense. Positioned in the middle of the field, she must have stamina for continuous running.

Open: A player who is not being marked or covered by a member of the opposing team is open.

Passing: Kicking the ball to a teammate.

Referee: An official who ensures the safety of all the players by enforcing the rules during a game.

Save: The prevention of an attempted goal, usually by the goalkeeper.

Scrimmage: A practice game.

Short-sided: A short-sided game is played with fewer than eleven players per team.

Substitution break: A quick break during which the coaches can put in new players and the players can grab a sip of water. Substitution breaks come a quarter and three quarters of the way through a game.

Throw-in: When the ball crosses the touchline, it is thrown back onto the field by a member of the team that did not touch the ball last. The thrower must keep both feet on or behind the touchline and throw the ball over her head.

Touchlines: Out-of-bounds lines that run along the long edges of the field.

Trapping: Gaining control of the ball using feet, thighs, or chest.